STEPS TO NOWHERE

Constance Leonard

The silent telephone caller, the unknown man lurking across the street from their Manhattan apartment—David Ingstrom refused to take them seriously. But even if Janie, his wife, was dramatizing ordinary occurrences, she had been strangely remote and unhappy for several weeks. Reason enough to accept their psychiatrist friend's recommendation that they take a holiday in Spain because Janie had lived there as a child and knew the language. It would be a second honeymoon. Their five year old son Aaron would be well cared for at home by the faithful Benita, who had once been Janie's nursemaid.

But Spain turned out to be a grim mistake. Soon, long-buried memories returned to terrify Janie, to cast their shadow on the present. And then came news of the mysterious disappearance of Benita and Aaron.

Here, set on the coast of Spain and in New York City, is the chilling story of a young woman who retraces her steps into the past and finds herself reliving an eerie and terrible experience.

Also by Constance Leonard

To be published by
MILTON HOUSE BOOKS

The other Maritha

STEPS TO NOWHERE

Constance Leonard

MILTON HOUSE BOOKS

MILTON HOUSE BOOKS
The Dolphin Publishing Co. Limited
at the Sign of the Dolphin
Milton Road, Aylesbury, HP21 7TH
England.

Editorial 26 Parkway, London NW1

*First published in 1974
by Dodd, Mead & Co., New York*

First Milton House Edition 1974

ISBN 0 85940 064 6

Printed in Great Britain by Alden & Mowbray Ltd
at the Alden Press, Oxford

Earlier . . .

The damp brown sand was hard-packed down near the edge of the water so that the child often ran there in the cleared space below the tide's leavings. Later she would be allowed to swim, but the spring days were treacherous, and the water that washed against the northern shore of Spain was cold still.

The land rose abruptly behind the beach and was top-heavy with great square houses, many of them empty now and blank-faced with their shades down, waiting for summer or for the war in Europe to end.

At one end of the long beach, in the far northern curve of the bay, the tiny white plaster houses of the Old Port snuggled into the cliff. The child was not to go there alone, nor to the narrow stone breakwater that pointed away from the other end of the beach like a long finger with a tiny lighthouse sparkling at its tip. There seemed to be a great deal of stonework—solid piers and seawalls built to withstand the surging water, and massive, reaching walls to hold back the land—all sheltering the beach in a harsh and overbearing way.

It was a good, wide place to play, but lonely. Janie did not know other American children in Bilbao, where her father was Consul. The British Consul's children were infants. She was nearly seven, old enough for school, although her mother gave her lessons at home every morning. And in the afternoons, after siesta, the youngest maid would take her for a walk, down the steep-pitched path to the beach. But Benita was in love with a seaman from Santander, and whenever Luis was around, she wanted to lag behind on a grassy slope above the beach, out of sight of the Civil Guard.

"You run along, chica, and chatter with the Guardia. I'll watch you from here," Benita said. Her brown, wet-chestnut eyes were unusually shiny that day.

"You think he's going to ask you to marry him," Janie accused her, not pleased to be shoved off, but she went, scuffing a track through the sand.

The noise grew enormous very suddenly. From a distant buzz that was indistinguishable from the constant muttering of the ocean, it became a monstrous hurtful thing that surrounded her. Squatting at the edge of the water, drawing pictures with a stick, Janie did not look up at all at first, not until the plane was low over the bay, skimming in like a giant gull, coming at her so close that she was engulfed in the roar and flattened onto the clammy sand.

The explosion seemed to shake everything loose—walls, houses, the entire world, so that Janie waited in terror for the beach to close over her and bury her alive, or the sea to roll in and drown her. When she at last dared to raise her head, she protected her face with both hands and peeked between her fingers to watch with a joyous kind of horror.

She forgot about Benita until the frantic voice, the "Chainee, Chainee," could not be ignored and Benita was wailing, "Oh, my God," and clutching at her.

Janie wrenched herself free, kicking desperately. "Can't you even say my name right!" she said.

Chapter 1

"And then there were just these stairs going on up . . . nowhere. With nowhere to go. It was the damnedest thing," Don Emmet said in awe and laughed quickly, embarrassed, as if he had witnessed something indecent. His laugh hung in the silence.

Jane Ingstrom turned toward him, her face drawn into a puzzled frown. "That's funny. Odd," she murmured. She had been standing at the far side of her living room talking to Lynn Brandt's husband, the handsome psychiatrist who reminded her of a blue jay. It was his slick *en brosse* hair and intense blue suits, and a habit he had of cocking his head, as he did now, attentively.

"Something wrong?"

"No, no." She shook off the question. "I don't think so. It's just . . ." She gave up and, turning her back on him, crossed the room. "What stairs, Don? Where did you see them?" she asked then, looking up at Don as if his answer mattered terribly.

Until then David Ingstrom would have said that the evening was going well, that Janie was fine, her old self again, the strange dark mood of the last few weeks forgotten. Certainly she was looking great. He liked the swing of her Chinese red palazzo pants and the silky clinging top. And tonight—maybe it was Dody Emmet's influence—she had been laughing a lot, giggling even, from the moment of Dody's disorganized arrival.

Dody could always make people laugh. Big-hearted, generous—to a fault, David believed the expression was—she had arrived spilling over with gifts, a marvelously wrapped pile of them toppling out of control. Packets of travel soap, as it turned out, and a heavy brass trivet and a magnificent box of crayons as a consolation prize for Aaron.

"Enough to color the entire city of New York!" Janie said.

"The whole world!" Aaron shouted.

"You can make a picture two weeks long, everything you do while we're away! But, Dody, you shouldn't have done so much." Under her laughing protest, Janie had been visibly touched; her eyes were suddenly damp.

"Not that you need anything, that's for sure."

"We won't if you keep giving us everything," Janie had teased.

Dody was instantly defensive, flustered by her own warm impulses. "Well, it is your anniversary, isn't it, your seventh? That's why the brass thing: brass for the seventh. At least that's what it says in my book. And you're going on a trip, aren't you?"

"We just wanted to see *you,* and show you the apartment, you know, before we took off."

"On a second honeymoon," Dody had sighed.

5

They had been neighbors on Riverside Drive. Even in mirror-image apartments with hardly a hair's difference between them, Dody had managed to make the Ingstroms sound enormously advantaged. And now, prowling the living room, admiring everything, she said, "You like it a whole lot better over here on the East Side, don't you?"

Do we? David wondered, thinking how Janie had been these last few weeks . . . how, unaccountably, she had changed, how her normal gaiety and enthusiasm seemed to have drained away. More than once she had looked lost, strangely silent and solitary. And apprehensive, so that without understanding he had wanted to comfort her, to hold onto her. It was as if she were slipping away from him and he had to pull her back.

"I don't know," he said. "The vibrations here . . ."

"Have got to be better," Dody insisted. "It's all so gorgeous, the furnishings, everything."

Janie had laughed and hugged her, "Dody, we've missed you," then extended a welcoming hand to each of the Brandts.

David straightened his shoulders and his glasses in an uneasy reflex that Nat Brandt often inspired. He suspected that Nat heard more than was being said, from professional habit, and saw beneath surfaces, just as David himself watched television commercials more analytically than most people.

Nat was years older than they were, of course, and European, Janie had pointed out, as if that explained everything, which it did not. David often wondered why Nat had got into psychiatry in the first place, what it was about his own life . . .

Nat scanned the room without comment, his eyes dark and mobile. Again David thought of the jay image and wished that Janie had never mentioned birds, because inevitably he had begun to see Lynn Brandt as a pigeon: sallow and full-busted, with pink-rimmed eyes. It was hard to believe that she and Janie had been school friends, they were so unlike, Lynn big-boned and remarkably matronly in appearance, Janie tiny by comparison and light and quick, her small face lively as a child's. Until recently anyway; only lately had the wariness come into her expression, and the hurt look.

"How very nice," Lynn said, blinking gently at the Emmets and then past them at the room itself. "Yes, lovely. And you're really off to Spain, Janie?"

"Some people have it all," Dody said. "I should be so lucky. If I had someone like Benny to take care of my kids . . ." She made a passionate clown's face and turned on Janie. "And you've been before, unfair!"

Janie laughed. "Not since I was a child, a million years ago! I wasn't much older than Aaron. And I hardly remember it, we moved around so much. All this . . ." She gestured widely at the wrought-iron candle sconces and silver roosters and the ubiquitous ceramics that gave the apartment its Latin feeling. "All this stuff belongs to my parents really. Like Benita and the whole setup. David and I just sort of inherited it when my father decided to retire to California. . . . David, darling, the Brandts need a drink! Lynn, dear, what would you like?"

There were just the six of them for dinner, and Aaron, in pajamas and bathrobe, passing a tilted bowl of black olives at knee height. Methodically, as an olive would roll onto the rug, the boy squatted and tidily transferred it to his mouth. David, waiting for drink orders, ruffled his son's hair. Lynn Brandt's attention wandered after his hand as she said, "Oh, anything, David. Scotch, I guess, thanks. With water."

She continued to watch Aaron with the doting, fussy absorption of the childless. Dody, having three of her own at home, was warmly offhand and capable of ignoring him.

"Angel, I wouldn't, not from the floor," Lynn worried, her face puckering, as Aaron secured another errant olive. "Dirty," she said.

Obscurely, as he poured her drink, David wished that Lynn were not Aaron's godmother. She was Janie's choice, because of long friendship—not that it matters, Janie would have assured him; it's an honorary position, godmothers don't *do* anything except give the odd present, unless they're needed, of course, if something happens to the parents. He was probably being unfair, unkind, he decided. "There you are, Lynn, Scotch for you."

She accepted the glass absently.

It was later, at the beginning of a second round of drinks, that Don Emmet's voice carried across the room and drew Janie to him. "Where, Don?" she probed with that strange earnestness.

"Where?" He paused, trying to be exact. "I was on my way up here, down around Fifty-first or Fifty-second, I think it was, and they were wrecking a building. With one of those wrecking balls, you know? It must have let fly just before I got there. Anyway, the street was jammed with people, and there was this great gaping place with the roof gone and the front wall and the top floor sheared off. And the stairs . . ."

"It sounds like a bomb site," Nat Brandt put in. "You'd see houses opened up like that during the war, cross sections. Almost like dolls' houses. You could see the wallpaper, and sometimes there'd be furniture. I remember a table with a cloth . . ."

"And stairs leading nowhere," Janie repeated, puzzled.

"You've seen this? No, of course, you're too young," Nat corrected himself, canting his head at her. "But it reminds you of something. It means something to you."

"Yes. Yes, I think it does," Janie said slowly. "But I don't know what. Isn't it annoying? I can't remember."

"Perhaps you don't really want to?" Nat suggested very gently, smiling.

Dody Emmet was matter-of-fact. "It's too morbid. Spooky. This whole town's getting spooky, if you ask me. The things that go on, the things you hear."

"What things?" Janie's voice sharpened. "What have you heard?"

David bent down to Aaron. "Maybe Benny has something else for you to pass. In the kitchen," he said.

"You know what I mean." Dody floundered until Aaron had left. "The things you read about all the time, the stabbing and the mugging and the stealing, all the violence. It's got so I'm looking behind me so much I'm always falling over things. And I'm not so crazy about taking the kids to the park either."

Janie nodded miserably. "At least I'm not the only one. David laughs at me. He thinks I made it all up out of my own private neuroses. Or whatever," with an uncertain smile in Nat Brandt's direction. "He doesn't believe that a man would keep staring at me."

"That's not quite what I said."

"Or wait across the street then, watching the entrance. Just because you've never seen him."

"I wouldn't take it so personally, that's all, living in an apartment house. He could be waiting for anybody. Maybe he lives over there."

"Then what about the telephone calls?"

"What telephone calls?" Dody wanted to know.

"I don't know who it is. That's the trouble. Whoever it is doesn't say anything."

"A wrong number?" Nat said. "Or a mechanical problem. They're common enough these days. Irritating, but better than threats or obscenity."

"Could be," Janie said, unconvinced. "But I think he's finding out if there's anyone at home."

"He?"

"All right, it. Or she. They never speak, they just hang up. And then they try again later."

David did not know how long Benita had been silently in the doorway, like an old Spanish carving with her hair drawn smooth on her scalp and her eyes hooded. When he looked at her, she moved her head back and forth slowly several times. Then in her careful English she said, "Is ready the dinner in the dining room."

The paella was saffron, steaming, laden with chicken and shrimp and chorizos. "And no bones, you'll be glad." Janie sat at the end of the table between Nat and Don with the candlelight shining on her pale hair and flushed cheeks. She looked fine again, at least at first. "Benny makes civilized paella. I remember, when I was little, the horror of finding chicken bones all mixed up with the rice. Or fish bones." She raised her wine glass. *"Buen provecho."*

Practiced at monitoring two sets at once, David half heard Dody Emmet. She talked a great deal of nonsense always, but her good-hearted envy was cheerful and flattering; David could almost believe that he and Janie did indeed have everything. But everything, according to Dody. Lynn Brandt, on his other side, listened with a faint, unwavering smile. An odd woman, David thought again.

"And by this time tomorrow night," Dody rounded her eyes. "Just think, David. You'll be on your way."

"I hope," he answered briefly, his attention diverted.

Janie had put down her fork with a look of exhaustion, as if the pretense of enjoying her food had become too great an effort. There was a flicker of confusion in her face, and as she leaned toward Nat Brandt—maybe it was a trick of the candlelight—her cheeks were deeply shadowed, hollowed, as if sucked in like a child's.

David started to say something. His first impulse was to reassure her, she looked so desolate. And then he was annoyed—with Janie for being unreasonably fearful; with himself for letting her worry him this way.

Nat was talking. "Dear lady, it is natural, a certain amount of anxiety." He was at ease with the subject, shaping it with his big hands, smiling. "Lord knows, in these times, anyone with an ounce of imagination . . . that's not to say that you are imagining . . . of sensitivity, I should say, great sensitivity.

"Why, I knew a case, a woman—an exquisite and extremely sensitive young woman, like yourself—who was

11

made ill by the atmosphere in her new apartment. Mind you, to all outward appearances, it was a charming place, and it was very costly. She had taken a long lease. But she could not live there. She suffered severe depression. She could not sleep. Perhaps, I thought, an allergy, dust, mold, something in the air. But no."

"Ghosts." Don Emmet laughed and washed down paella with a gulp of wine. "You hear about haunted houses all the time. How about haunted apartments?"

"Exactly." Nat's head moved up and down somewhat ponderously. "An aura of evil, she called it, and this, on investigation, was not at all fanciful. There was, there frequently is, a physical explanation, too. Simple enough, once it has been exposed.

"Here, too, the telephone played a part. There were calls at all hours in the night. Unpleasant calls, insinuations, vicious words that were intolerable to a fastidious woman. She felt soiled, contaminated. She came to believe that these calls were intended for her. They were not, of course. By an oversight, the telephone number had been left unchanged when she moved into the apartment. The calls were intended for the previous tenant, who was also a single lady.

"No, perhaps not a lady." Nat smiled modestly. "A woman of some notoriety, it was learned, the mistress, girlfriend, however you call it, of a fairly successful hoodlum."

"Gangster's moll," Don supplied.

Nat bowed. "Precisely. Until his untimely death. There seemed, in fact, to have been a number of sudden and somewhat violent deaths, at least one of them directly associated with the apartment in question."

"And this woman you knew sensed all that? Wow!" said Don.

"She had a rare sensitivity. Some people do. It's as if their perceptions are heightened, more acute than most. . . ." Nat leaned toward Janie, flattering her.

It was David's turn to laugh. "Terrific. So that's why Janie's picking up all these weird vibrations. Well, well, sweetie, what have your old mom and dad been up to!"

Nat laughed too, doubtfully. "You understand, this is only an example I have given you. I do not mean to suggest . . . good Lord, no." He turned back to Janie abjectly, hunched, his attitude, as David saw it, very much that of a predatory bird.

"Anyway, I don't go in for that psychic business," Janie told him. "I never have premonitions, ESP, any of that. I have a very pedestrian mind really, very workaday."

"Dear lady, that I would never say. The human mind has limitless capabilities, infinite . . ."

"Then we shouldn't leave," Janie went on. "If there's something wrong with the apartment, if that's the message I'm getting, I can't leave Aaron here. I'd feel guilty . . ."

"No, no," Nat protested. That was not at all what he had meant; he had chosen a foolish example. "Of course, you must go . . . have your holiday, it is the best thing. You must never take counsel from your fears, remember." His smile was soft, placating. "And you must not feel guilty, no. That is very bad for people, having feelings of guilt. . . ."

The voice itself was balm—not at all like a blue jay's, David decided, but warm and deep, sensual as all hell. Like hot lather, for God's sake. He abruptly disliked Nat Brandt's

13

phrasing and the faint German accent that persisted after all these years. And gave him class, like the unnameable sculpture in his waiting room?

David's resentment burgeoned at the thought of Nat's office. It was his own fault, his own idea to consult Nat about Janie. He had regretted the impulse at once, feeling disloyal and diminished and coldly exposed in the expensive office. What he felt about Janie was a private matter, much too personal and too special somehow to be aired there.

Not that Nat hadn't been benevolence itself, wedging him in between two lucrative patients. "Since I don't really go in for marriage counseling per se"—the controlled smile—"and there are a great many books on the subject . . ."

"I just thought, since you've known Janie for a long time . . . how she is normally, that is, or how she was . . ."

"She's certainly not an hysterical type. No, on the contrary. I would have said extremely well adjusted . . . happy," deprecating the simple layman's terms. "The tension you describe doesn't sound like her, the remoteness. Nor the baseless fear."

"At this point I almost wish there were some real threat, something I could get my hands on. This way . . ."

Nat had smiled slightly. "But there's absolutely nothing in it, you're certain of that, no sinister character?"

"Not that I've seen. If there were, I wouldn't have bothered you. I'd have gone to the police."

"Yes, naturally." Nat did not take offense. "And the same is true of the mysterious calls. You're convinced that Janie is dramatizing an ordinary occurrence."

"They don't happen when I'm around, I know that. And Benny's there all the time. She'd know if there was anything

14

funny going on. She says there isn't."

The large blue jay head tilted. "And before? Before this started, you and Janie were fine, you had a good marriage?"

"Before we moved." When David thought about it, they had been very happy in their first apartment. There was a moral in there somewhere, something to do with the simple virtues and the curse of unearned luxury. He made a face and abandoned the thought. "Sure. Great," he said.

"There's no one else, nothing like that? You and Janie love each other?" The question had sounded unprofessional, impertinent.

The trip, too, was Nat's idea, their getting off by themselves for a change, although Nat had a talent for letting his patients feel that they had arrived at their own solutions. "How long since you've had a real holiday, just the two of you? Exactly," Nat had said knowingly. David had been too occupied with his advertising, hadn't he, and Janie with Aaron, or with her parents all the past summer, helping them move? But away from all this, free as air, just the two of them—Nat had thrown up his hands in a joyful, balloon-tossing gesture—there seemed to be no limit to their idyllic prospects.

"Now that Aaron is in nursery school," Nat clinched matters on a practical level, "and you have reliable help . . ."

"Benny? She's been with the Vreelands since Janie was little, ever since they were in Spain. She's a member of the family."

Maybe that was how Spain came into it. David was never sure whose idea Spain was and that Janie would be thrilled to go back. Back to a familiar country where she would know the language, Nat had pointed out.

"I don't know," David had hesitated. "I don't know how much she remembers. She never talks about it much. At least she didn't, until lately," he corrected himself. "Maybe it's being back in her family's apartment with all that Spanish stuff to remind her. And Benny."

"It will all come rushing back to her. She will regain her childhood, her youth!" Nat showed his pleasure at this upbeat and punctual conclusion.

"I'd just as soon Janie didn't know," David said quickly as he was eased out the door. "About my being here, I mean. She'd take it the wrong way. You can see why, the implications."

"Of course." Nat had nodded, and now, at the other end of the table, his handsome head inclined toward Janie, he was again nodding agreeably. "Absolutely, dear lady. For that reason, too, it is good that you are going. It would be the worst thing, to let your own anxiety affect your son."

"Right," Don Emmet concurred, chewing. He had a part interest in a sporting goods store and a wholesome, physical fitness approach.

"Children are uncannily perceptive," Nat added.

"But then how do we teach them? Not fear—I don't want to frighten Aaron—but caution, for his own protection."

"Ahh . . ." said Nat.

But David missed the rest as Dody Emmet burbled on his left, ". . . too perfect. Honestly, David, some people have all the luck."

Surreptitiously, with a mere tap of a middle finger on the table, David touched wood. He wondered what the devil had got into him; he had never done such a thing before.

16

Chapter 2

There has got to be a point of no return somewhere along here, David thought in Queens, in the taxi approaching Kennedy Airport. Beyond a given number of miles or minutes from home it must be too late to worry about what you forgot to pack. Or lock. Or turn off. Having gone through his pockets and found tickets, passport, money, everything in order, he was ready to look ahead to the trip itself. Certainly he had had no qualms about abandoning the Digby account; their new line of lotions and potions could muddle along without him for a couple of weeks—or go hang.

He stretched and settled back into the seat, ready to enjoy himself. Fondly, exasperated, he pulled Janie back with him. She was fussing beyond reasonable limits. Aaron's small face, like his ubiquitous red Jell-O, seemed to have come with them.

"It's just that I've never left him for so long. Or gone so far, you know?" Janie rubbed at a sticky spot on her cheek. "You do think it's all right, David. You're sure?"

"With Benny in charge, old eagle eye herself?"

"I know, but . . ."

"You trust her."

"Yes."

Why did he hear doubt? "It's not as if we'd got her out of the want ads," he said. "We know that she's honest. And reliable—good Lord, she'd guard that little boy with her life. And she's not a secret tippler or anything like that."

"No." Again Janie managed to stretch the word. "But she has other problems. The language, for one. She doesn't always understand, you know, and sometimes she has trouble making herself clear. What if something did go wrong, if she needed help?"

"She knows how to reach your mother and father, doesn't she? She has their California number. She can always scream at them in Spanish if she has to."

In the boarding area—what did they call it now, the sanitized area?—Janie's thoughts came back around again, full circle. The new security procedures did not interest her. Bemused, she submitted to the metal detector and surrendered her handbag. When she had been cleared and there was no turning back, when a frantic retreat to a telephone booth might have triggered unimaginable repercussions, she worried: "At least, I think I left that number by the phone in the kitchen. I'm almost certain."

David's patience was frayed. "You know damned well you did. And our hotel in Madrid. And the Emmets' number and the Brandts' and for all I know the FBI and the Secret Service. For God's sake, Janie, we're only going to be gone a couple of weeks."

Still, they had been at cruising altitude for some time and were well over the Atlantic before Janie managed to wrench herself altogether out of the apartment. Their drinks had arrived, and food threatened imminently on some unsettling middle-of-the-black-night schedule designed, David speculated, to condition their stomachs to Spanish mealtimes. Janie looked around with a vague air of pleasant surprise.

He said, "Welcome aboard," and raised his glass.

"We're really going. After all these years. I don't think I believed it quite. It was all so long ago, Spain, all that, it was as if it was gone for good, like my childhood." She laughed at herself. "But it's a lovely idea, a lovely present. Thank you, darling," she said formally, raising her glass. *"Buen viaje.* What's so damned funny?"

"You. You always were a hard one to seduce. You always wanted a hell of a lot of persuading to do what you really wanted to do in the first place."

"But it was well worth your trouble. That's what you always said, anyway." She could not suppress a wide, merry grin. "Now if you'd like to go to the trouble of kissing me . . ."

Several times through that night, David thought of Nat Brandt with a grudging kind of gratitude. Nat could be right, it was good to get away—out of the rut, to coin a phrase. Already, in a matter of a few hundred miles, Janie had lost her strained look.

The plane itself offered neutral distractions, other routines. Janie had always loved to fly. As a child she had traveled a great deal with her parents, but she had hardly been out of New York for the past seven years. Since their honeymoon in Bermuda their travels had taken them no farther than New England or the Jersey shore.

She took a childlike interest now in the small amenities

of flight as if they were forgotten toys, rediscovered. The miniature liquor bottles appealed to her, and although she was not hungry she was taken with the appointments of her tray and the stewardesses' constant offerings. After supper she adjusted herself for the night with every sign of contentment, turned off the air valve and light, folded away the armrest and nestled under David's arm. Amused, he thought of the sex appeal in the airlines' commercials and wondered if there might be some truth in advertising after all.

Neither of them slept exactly, but they dozed and talked in a drifty way about whatever floated to mind. There was a closeness about the darkened cabin and the enveloping noise of the engines; they found themselves reminiscing and confiding—with the ease of people who had only just met, David thought once, wryly.

Oddly assorted memories, fragments of other trips, surfaced. For the first time in years David thought of a bus ride he had taken through Minnesota with his grandfather, north to go fishing. And he remembered flying home at the time of his mother's death, being stacked up over Minneapolis in a snowstorm, circling in wide, woozy loops until they could land at last on a surreal, cotton wool runway.

"Funny," Janie murmured. "I think of Spain as all brown. Sepia, faded, like old photographs of my mother's. But nothing to do with me. It's as if I'd never been there myself, only told about it. As if I didn't remember any of it personally, at first hand."

"I know that feeling. Sometimes it's hard to be sure . . ."

"They say we shut out what we don't want to remember."

"Could be." David smiled, suddenly wanting to lighten the mood. "Though I distinctly remember a dancing class

I was shanghaied into."

Janie did not seem to hear him. Behind closed eyes she was apparently pursuing some idea of her own.

"Nat says memory is terribly significant. It's what people don't talk about that counts. What they bury deepest . . ."

She was asleep when dawn streaked across the horizon ahead of them. It was later, as they came down toward Madrid and she saw the first of the brown-green wind-molded plateaus, that she said, "Yes. Of course. That is how it was in color. I'm beginning to remember."

"How what was?"

The question seemed to puzzle her. Or perhaps, her ears filled by the plane's quick descent, she hadn't heard. In either case, she did not answer.

On his own David would have approached Madrid without any personal, emotional commitment, simply as a first-time tourist. Janie shuddered. She had visions of open-necked sport shirts hung round with cameras, great docile herds of them being told where to look and what to think.

"Of course, if you'd rather be in a group . . ." She spun out the pause happily, teasing, being funny and happy about sex as she hadn't for a long time. "I mean, if you'd rather be in a tour group." She stretched back on the bed in their hotel room, arms angled under her head, doing The Nude Maja. They had just seen the Goyas in the Prado, although *seen* was too easy a word for Janie's rapt involvement, her transfixed stance as dark and violent scenes swirled around her and demanded all her senses. They would save the rest of the museum for another day.

David followed along wherever Janie wanted to go—the shops, the palaces, the discotheques. The rhythms of the

Spanish day were strange—he could not imagine how anyone did a day's work here when the entire city virtually closed every afternoon—but he was happy enough to be led, to let Janie plan their itineraries and their meals, to let her decipher the enormous menus, groping through her memory of the language, and to go to bed with her after lunch for a leisurely siesta. They had never been more compatible. It was as if they had been physically separated for a long time.

"It's all the lovely wine," Janie said, flushing.

"Or something." He was thinking of the privacy they had not had since Aaron learned to toddle.

They wrote postcards home every day for the first three days at a kiosk near the post office where they drank coffee and watched a fountain leap into the morning sun.

With a sense of truancy—of guilt almost—they walked childless in Retiro Park, having only each other's hands to hold, like young lovers. Yellowing leaves on the paths and brilliant beds of marigolds seemed to radiate the glowing warmth of the October day.

"Not bad," David said. "Give me about three more seconds, I think I could adjust to this life. I'm very adaptable."

Janie slipped her hand under his arm. "You're wonderful. Mind going back to the Prado for a while, now that we're practically there? Last chance, if we're going north tomorrow."

He went cheerfully, with no sense of foreboding at all. Janie was not one to overdo this sort of thing; she was a selective viewer, and she bypassed the Goyas this time, heading directly upstairs to the Velázquez rooms.

It was a dramatic collection, tremendous in its vitality

and the variety of life overflowing the canvases. Even to an untrained eye, the impact was inescapable. There was something about the long-dead royal children, the tiny, haughty Infanta among her maids in waiting, and the little doomed Don Carlos so arrogantly astride his horse, riding on top of the world, no older than Aaron. For a moment David saw Aaron in the fancy-dress costume, and then he moved on slowly to the marvelously drunken faces of the Borrachos.

Surely nobody needed a translation, yet there was one eager American who was apparently interested in nothing but the titles. David watched her joyfully for some time, the sneakered bent-kneed approach to the name plaques, the close peering, the riffling of the pages of her dictionary, before she moved on avidly to the next without once, so far as David could see, really looking up at the paintings.

Janie touched his arm. "David . . ." She was whispering, but not because the museum demanded a reverent hush. She had a shocked, wide-eyed look and as she pulled him along after her, he thought at first that she must be feeling sick. It took him a minute to understand that it was a painting she wanted him to see.

"David, look! There on the right, by the horse. Who does that look like?"

It was a vast military scene, the famous Surrender of Breda, with the raised lances, straight as masts, prominent in the background. The Spanish soldiers were grouped at the right, each of the strong faces an individual portrait, tough and proud and extraordinarily lifelike.

"You see the one who's looking this way, as if he's looking at me?" Janie's voice was guarded still, as if the man could not only see her but hear her. "Doesn't he remind you of someone?"

David studied the face for some time, playing along, and at last said, "Okay, I'll bite. Not knowing many Spaniards, I'll guess Benny. Is that what you're getting at?"

"Exactly!" Janie triumphed. "Enough like her to be her brother. He also looks like the man in New York, the one who was lurking across the street. Why I didn't see that . . .!"

She was not being funny. Just for a moment David could hope that she was, that she was laughing at herself, that she had got over her silly fear and that this was her oblique and nutty way of saying so. But there was no apology in the bite of her fingernails into his wrist and no humor about her mouth.

"You have that character on the brain!"

She would not let him off the subject so lightly. "Don't you see?"

"Frankly, no. Just because one Spaniard looks like another, or reminds you of someone else . . . What do you want me to do, rush a description to the New York Police? I've got an even better idea. Send them one of those postcard reproductions. Mug shot by Velázquez. They'd love it."

"Oh, David. Think a minute. What if it is her brother?"

"Okay, what if it is? I suppose he's got as much right as anyone else to be on Seventy-second Street. More, if he came to see his sister."

"From across the street?"

"Poor guy," David said. He was beginning to enjoy the subject. "Maybe he's shy. You're sure it is her brother, not her boyfriend?"

"Her boyfriend died."

The flat statement, made with a somehow disproportionate grimness, stopped him for a moment. "Sorry."

"A long time ago," Janie said.

"Well, then, if it is her brother . . ." The decent interval over, he went on in a practical tone. "You know how siblings are. He probably wasn't sure of his welcome. Or was it you he was afraid of? If there's something between you two . . ." He took off on this line of conjecture playfully, but Janie seemed unaware. She was somewhere far away and out of earshot.

"Hell," he said finally. "I didn't even know she had a brother."

"Oh, she had one, all right," Janie said then with bitterness. "Manolo. But he's not supposed to be in New York.

"Janie, darling, look. Please. It's not worth getting all upset about."

"I'm sorry. I can't explain. But I've got to call home."

She hurried away, not looking back to see if he was following.

Only the American lady with the dictionary heard him mutter, "Damn it to hell," which she took badly in the circumstances as a desecration. His low opinion of Dr. Nathaniel Brandt's professional competence he kept to himself.

Chapter 3

In New York it was morning still of a warming October day with an obscure sun somewhere behind the amber haze.

Benita walked as if her feet hurt, in no hurry to go back to the apartment now that the boy was safely in school. The boy, he was the important thing. Fierce, inexpressible feeling made her eyes ache until the veins reddened and an ugly tear formed.

She was not fifty yet, but she looked older, graying, so that she had thought sometimes that she might be mistaken for Aaron's grandmother. Except for the boy's coloring, of course; he had his mother's very fair skin and hair. But Benita was well enough dressed. Her coat was, in fact, a gift from Aaron's grandmother, a good nubbly black wool one that Mrs. Vreeland said she would never need again, not in California. Never wear black again . . . for mourning, for old age? In her superstitious mind fragments of prayers formed and her lips moved, but she caught herself and stopped that, not wanting people to think that she was some crazy woman.

The shop windows were only an excuse to loiter. She was certainly not in a mood to buy anything, but from habit she turned toward the display of goods and watched her own reflection and the people moving behind her on the sidewalk, mirrored in the glass.

The food store where she did most of the marketing and the delicatessen marked the beginning of her own neighborhood—her own village, as she thought of it after so many years. She had a wide acquaintance among the grocery boys and doormen, wide but all on the surface. For all the times they had spoken, she could not have said where most of them lived or if they loved their wives, or even if they had children. And she did not feel that she could turn to any one of them now for help.

A good smell of sawdust and sausages came through the open door of the delicatessen. The cluttered windows gave off no clear reflection, only the price of cold cuts and grinders and macaroni salad. Not that it mattered . . . her eyes were blurred. Her heart was pounding so, it was as if the blood throbbed in her eyes. This time he was not going to have his own way. He was not going to get what he wanted. She had so little . . .

"Where are they, Benita?" The evil, whispered insinuations on the telephone. "There are more, aren't there? Jane has them, doesn't she? Unless you stole them, Benita?"

He had forced her to lie. It was certain that she could not explain the telephone calls to Jane's husband.

"Then I'll have to find out for myself, true, Benita?"

She walked on, her head swinging back and forth slowly like an old turtle's.

The apartment house was an early cooperative built of buff stucco and blackened oak. It was this obscure Spanish derivation as much as the solid, old-fashioned construction that had attracted the Vreelands. The walls were thick and muffling, the corridors wide and carpeted, and the prevailing odor was of camphor.

The lobby was empty when Benita went in. The doorman, according to the indicator above the closed elevator door, was on the fifth floor. She went on through to the service stairs and climbed them slowly, holding onto the railing. When she reached the third floor, she was panting slightly and rested for a moment before she pushed open the heavy door into the hall. Above her own breathing she could hear the hum of the descending elevator, then nothing but a total boxed-in silence.

She had had the key in her pocket, clenched in her hand, and now she turned it in the lock quietly, as if it were important to maintain the silence. The well-built door swung easily into a small, shadowy foyer.

Here the disorder was hardly noticeable. The one drawer of the narrow commode, where Mrs. Vreeland had kept her gloves and Jane had crammed a jumble of scarves and mittens, was not quite closed. Benita tucked in the fringe of a scarf.

In the deep living room with its bright wall of casement windows, her eyes adjusted slowly to the tumbled sofa cushions on the floor and the spilled contents of a desk. Books had been pulled every which way from their shelves and candlesticks overturned. Benita pressed her knuckles against her teeth as if to hold back moans. A pottery jardiniere, the large one that had held the avocado tree, lay on the white

Spanish rug, jagged bits of it among the exposed avocado roots and dark, moist earth. Benita could smell the dirt; she had watered it that morning.

It was in the dining room, which was small, hardly more than a passageway to the kitchen, that the devastation seemed worst. The contents of the sideboard overwhelmed the table, obscuring the polished surface except for some new scratches where the flannel silver bags had been dumped out and spoons and forks had skittered across the wood. Linens lay bunched on the floor like mounds of laundry waiting to be done, but with pitchers and vegetable dishes and salt cellars crazily among them.

Benita dropped to her knees beside a thick, felt-backed heraldic tile that had been used under hot dishes. It was cracked in two diagonally, so that only the glued felt held the halves loosely together. Bowed over it, her hands trembling, she fumbled with the blue and gold pieces of what had been the coat of arms of the city of Bilbao. She had never been sure what it all meant, the stone bridge or the two dogs, one of them in midair for no reason, or the three towers. Invicta Villa de Bilbao, it said.

She shivered. The lightning-shaped crack streaked across its face like a bad omen.

"Benita," he said from the hall behind her. "What took you so long?"

Chapter 4

Under other conditions David would have liked the Bilbao train. Even now, in a game effort to reopen communications with Janie, he went on about it at some length, exaggerating its virtues. He had never seen a compartmented, European-style train outside of the movies, so that from the first piping whistle everything about it evoked romance and intrigue. Or so he said, talking at Janie as he fingered the shiny mahogany and the green cut-plush upholstery. There were gilded luggage racks overhead and on each wall two framed photographs, pretty little landscapes, flanking a mirror.

"My God, 'The Lady Vanishes,' " he said, delighted.

Janie looked up at him bleakly.

"I'm sorry. I really am." He sat down next to her again to touch her, at least put his hand on her arm. "I didn't mean to say that. It just came out."

She continued to stare out the window at the worn green and brown plains. They were perhaps half an hour north of Madrid.

"Look, we'll call home again just as soon as we get somewhere. There's nothing to worry about, just because she wasn't there a couple of times. She had to take Aaron to school and go get him. Maybe buy some stuff," he improvised. "And if it's a nice day, they could've gone to the park. You know. And you've got to remember there's a time difference, it's hours earlier there. It's hard to keep in mind, isn't it? I mean that the sun gets here first, so they're having breakfast when we're having lunch . . ."

After several rounds of this he was beginning to feel that the record was stuck. Repetition was turning whatever he said into meaningless gobbledegook.

If they had been alone in the compartment, David thought, he would have taken Janie by the shoulders and shaken her until he cracked the brittle shell she was encased in, brooding and private. Or he would have put his arms around her and admitted that he was beginning to feel uneasy, too, just a little. Perhaps, comforted, she would have cried on his shoulder and told him what she did know, calmly and coherently.

But there was a young man sitting opposite them, dark and slick-haired, oddly contemporary in his yellow LaCoste turtleneck. He did not speak English. David had asked and been answered with a regretful smile. Still, his presence and his constant regard were off-putting, the way his eyes kept coming back to rest inevitably on Janie. Granted, he had a limited choice. He would look out the window for a time then, making rather a show of concentration, consult the map on his lap, but when he rested, eyes straight ahead, he stared at Janie.

She could hardly ignore him and in the end began to talk

to him in her rapidly returning Spanish, which excluded David altogether. Watching them and snatching at a recognizable word here and there, he could see how the language affected Janie, how it involved her hands and altered the pitch of her voice and animated her eyes. She was like an actress immersed in a new role, a role that was alien to David and widened the distance between them.

"The kid sure turns you on," he said. "How come so chummy with strangers all of a sudden? So trusting?"

"He works for the phone company. In Vizcaya. They're installing wide-range dialing," she elaborated coolly.

David was more than ready for the lunch announcement when it came. With Janie translating and explaining the system, he took tickets for the first seating.

The swaying dining car was a pleasure in itself, dark-paneled, fragrant, filled with starched linen and genial waiters and nostalgia for forgotten trips. "The first time I took a train to Chicago, let me tell you," David began and, laughing, put his hand over Janie's on the table. "Peace? Then I'll spare you my memoirs, which on second thought didn't hold a candle to this anyway. How about some *vino?*"

They sat opposite each other at a table by themselves, freed from Janie's telephone company friend. The jounce and hustle of the train were evident here, making a pleasant slosh in the mineral water bottle and a challenge of the wine, a matter of due attention to the eccentric rhythms of the car. Plate after plate was dealt to them—crusty bread, antipasto, Spanish tortillas, steaks—while the countryside rushed past, a changed view now of vineyards and sheep and here and there a plow drawn by oxen. Something about the scrabbly, difficult land and flicks of rain slanting across the windows served to heighten the sense of privilege and plenty inside.

"It's going to be all right," David said warmly. "There's usually a simple explanation of these things, you know. And then we'll get back to what we were doing, like having fun, remember? That's the point of this exercise. Every day a holiday, every meal a banquet . . ."

Janie smiled back at him, tentatively. "You may be right."

"No doubt about it. You'll feel better when you've talked to Benny."

"Yes. Tonight. Tonight for sure. And I'll go see her father. I promised her I would. He'll know where Manolo is."

"Probably right where he belongs," David said, and as Janie bit her lip, "What's with this creep anyway? What did he do to you?"

She jabbed at her steak, then pushed it aside. "Lord, how I hated that boy! That's what I remember about him, a crawly feeling. He must have been sixteen or seventeen, about ten years older than I was, so we wouldn't have had much to do with each other when I lived here. I don't remember him clearly as a *person,* and he didn't molest me or anything like that, but there was something . . .

"Something wrong." Searching her memory, she had stared through David, blank-eyed. Now she leaned toward him with a strange intensity as if willing him to grasp something that eluded her. "Something unpleasant. Like a nasty taste. Do you know what I'm trying to say? I think he may have been retarded, not quite bright anyway. I don't remember his going to school or if he'd finished, only that he seemed to be around a lot. And he said he had to watch me.

That was it, that was his excuse, he said he had to watch me every minute because Benita told him to, whenever Luis was around. So that she and Luis could make love, I suppose, and Manolo probably spied on them, too—he was like that, sneaky—or made them pay him to stay away. I remember now, he had some sort of night job, washing dishes, I think, though I have an idea he made it sound a lot grander. He was full of grandiose schemes. I forget whether he was going to win the lottery or be a famous matador."

Her smile was more cynical than happy, but she leaned back and eased her shoulders as if this spate of memories had helped, as if some pressure had been released. With an air of regaining her bearings, she gave her attention to the harsh autumn landscape, the black-striped, smoking burned over fields and the abrupt rocky outcroppings.

"Neither of which quite happened to him, I gather," David prompted cautiously.

"No, of course not, and I don't know what did. Or care. Benny never talks about him. And I hadn't thought about him, not for years, not until this."

He interceded quickly before she could slip away from him again, "And what about Benny's great love? Luis, you called him."

"He's dead."

"So you said, but you didn't tell me what happened."

"He drowned. Isn't that ironic, a merchant seaman drowning?"

"They say a lot of fishermen don't know how to swim. Same idea, I suppose."

"Benny never believed it. They were going to be married, and then he died, just like that. I think that's why she stayed on with my family and left Bilbao with them."

Intently, with a child's total absorption, she worked at the breadcrumbs on the tablecloth, brushing them into a pile, aligning them with the side of her little finger. "Luis Varga," she said dreamily. "That was his name—Luis Varga. Isn't it funny how things are coming back to me, bit by bit, now that I'm back here? The closer we get to Bilbao, it seems. David . . ."

She lifted her hand and reached between their wine glasses as if she wanted to touch him or be held onto, but the waiter was there. She drew back and folded her hands primly in her lap while the table was crumbed and new plates were dealt out.

"Do you want cheese, pastry, or fruit?" she said. *"Queso, tarta o fruta,"* she enunciated in a high, clear singsong, and David realized what else it was that speaking Spanish did to Janie: it made her sound very young.

"Just coffee, thanks. I'm stuffed," he said, and then lightly, "As you were saying, sweetie . . .?"

"Nothing really." She looked helpless, as if he had asked too much. "I was just wondering. Do you think Nat's right . . . about our burying things so deeply that we hide them from ourselves, things we can't bear to remember?"

"I've heard that before—it's a psychological trick—that the mind can protect itself by forgetting some things, unpleasant things. Not forgetting exactly, but filing them away out of sight. As you say, burying them."

"Out of sight," Janie repeated. "But not out of mind. It's still there, isn't it? Whatever it was . . . it's there somewhere." She frowned with a strained, unseeing look.

"Then I suppose it will surface eventually—like a name

you've forgotten—when you're not trying so hard."

Janie stirred her coffee round and round as if she were winding something up. "But what if I don't want to remember? David . . . if it's something so awful . . . so awful that I can't bear to think about it ever?"

He took the spoon from her and put it in her saucer, then anchored her hand under his on the table. "Isn't it always better to know, to face things? Get the problem out where you can see it?" Abruptly he laughed at himself. "Now hear this: Dr. Ingstrom, psychiatrist, speaking! This is Nat's department, baby, not mine. But isn't that what analysis is about? Dredging deep into the subconscious . . .?"

"And the feeling of guilt. David . . . something happened here, I know it did, here in Spain. Something horrible. And I was involved somehow."

"Not you." He manipulated the tiny bones in her hand.

"And now that I'm back here . . ."

He felt her hand bunch into a tight fist. "Come on," he said uncomfortably, signaling for the check.

The enormous lunch and the warm, rocking compartment combined to stupefy David. He sank heavily into the corner of his seat and let his weighted eyes close. Random words set up a rhythm in his mind, words like "leaden torpor, leaden torpor" numbingly repeated until they were replaced by the inescapable commercials for American digestive aids.

Young LaCoste had apparently forgone lunch. He was wide awake and voluble, inordinately pleased to be reunited with Jane. La Peste, David thought, and wondered if he had thereby exhumed an actual French word from an otherwise wasted high school course . . . speaking of things long forgotten. Their voices wove in and out of David's vagrant consciousness. He had a sensation of floating, semi-detached, partially anesthetized, his head a balloon at the end of a long string. So that when Janie spoke directly to him, sharply and louder than necessary in her excitement, he felt misused, brought back with a jerk that snapped his neck.

"David, did you hear that?"

He rubbed the back of his head and looked stupidly at his watch, as if it would help to know how long he had been away.

"Did you hear what he said?"

He was not yet up to reminding her that hearing would not have helped in any case, since nine out of ten of the Spanish words ran together in his ears in a meaningless mush. He rubbed his face and resettled his glasses. "Okay, now, sweetheart, slowly, please, from the top."

With a trace of vengeance, Janie began by spacing every word, but she could not restrain herself for long. "We were talking about Bilbao," she said. "He's very knowledgeable, really. Of course, he would be in his line of work, about his own territory. Anyway, I was asking him about it, if there were a lot of changes—it's all so dim in my mind, really I was just making conversation, for practice. And somehow we got around to the area where I used to live. It's a suburb and sort of a summer resort, out on the beach. He says I may not recognize it, there's been such a lot of building, but the Old Port stays the same."

Janie laughed. "I don't think he goes much for quaint charm. He sounded a little ashamed of the Old Port, as if they should have modernized it, and he was anxious to tell me about a nice new hotel out that way. *Elegante,* you'll be glad to hear. I thought we might try it. Anyway, we got into a vague game of Do-you-know? since Benny's father still lives in the Old Port. I didn't really think he'd know the old man, but I thought he might have run into Manolo somewhere. He hadn't, *but* . . ." She paused for maximum effect.

"Ruffle of drums?" he murmured.

"It's unbelievable," she said as if he hadn't spoken. "We progressed from there to restaurants. I thought maybe he could recommend some, and he did, and then—are you ready?"

He nodded, with no great expectations, but beginning to enjoy Janie's presentation.

"He told me about a fish shack out on the beach. Well, not in those words exactly, but I gather it's a very plain place, the kind we might bypass. He sounded a little apologetic, but he often goes there because it's cheap and good, for seafood especially. It's called El Barco de Luis, and it's run by a retired sailor—naturally, with a name like that—a man by the name of Luis Varga."

David knew, from Janie's intense expectancy, that the punch line had come—and gone—without his getting it. For a second he questioned her need to wake him for this particular revelation, and then bit by bit he said, "Oh. Luis. You mean *that* Luis. The one Benny was going to marry. The dead one," stupidly.

Janie looked as if she had just discovered a new continent, both elated and fearful. "Isn't it incredible?"

That was the very word. "It must be a common name. Around here," he said doubtfully.

"That's what I thought, at first. I thought it was just a

funny coincidence. I mean, that would have been amazing enough, wouldn't it? But there's more." Her eyes were round and avid.

"Don't tell me he has a wife called Benita."

Janie's hair bounced as she shook her head. "No, but you're getting warm, in a way. I kept pumping our friend here . . ."

Smiled at and understanding that he was being talked about, LaCoste looked hopeful, but Janie went on with the story in English and David, for the first time, welcomed the language barrier.

". . . and it all fits," Janie continued. "This Luis, the restaurant man, is in his forties, which would be right, upper forties, and he was at sea for years and years. He never did marry." She grinned. "Not what you're thinking. Our friend was very man-of-the-world on that point. He imagines a lady in every port—Luis being that attractive, and still causing a few heart throbs. Anyway, he comes from somewhere along the coast. A family of fishermen, but he seems to be the last of them. And he settled out there at the beach not very long ago.

"Now, there is a rumor," Janie stressed each word, "that the reason he chose Bilbao is that he thinks it's lucky for him. He had been happy there once, long ago. There was a girl . . ."

"Janie," David began in a reasonable tone, "for God's sake . . ."

"Oh, I know. It's only a rumor, but rumors are often *based* on fact. They may get it all wrong and come out backwards in the end, but it takes a grain of truth somewhere to get them started. Luis must have hinted at something of the sort."

"Or said nothing at all, so that people were forced to make up a past for him. You know how people are. A good-looking guy turns up, a stranger, he's a sitting duck. Unless he tells all, people improvise. There's nothing like a romantic story on a dull day, but let's not get carried away. If by any chance this were Benita's Luis, someone should have made the connection. Wouldn't she have heard? Wouldn't someone have told her, her family or her friends?"

Janie considered for a minute, reaching back through the years. "Maybe not. I have an idea it was all a big secret . . . that her family might not have approved . . . maybe because he was a sailor and an outsider."

"What about her brother?"

"Oh, yes, he knew all about Luis. Manolo knew everything—he made a point of it. And he would recognize Luis if he saw him," she concluded unhappily; then, defiantly, "But it still could be him!"

"He," David amended with irritating accuracy.

Stubbornly she said, "It still could be Benita's old boyfriend."

"And if it turns out that you're right, then what?"

She had the nonplussed look of someone who has just won a tug of war. There was quite a long pause while she regrouped and then, her anger deflected to a new target, she said, "He's a real stinker, isn't he? An absolute bastard to break her heart that way, letting her think he was dead. If he didn't want to marry her, okay, but he didn't have to fake a drowning." She chewed on her lip, scowling. "Then what about his being so happy and that bit about the girl in Bilbao?"

David joined into the conjecture with a good deal of creative spirit. "I'd say he drowned all right and this is his ghost back haunting the scene."

She did not respond.

"Or there's reincarnation, if you prefer." Her troubled face stopped him. He would not have said that he was unduly sensitive to atmosphere, but at that moment the fun had gone out of the subject. The compartment seemed darker.

Outside, it was true, the rain was making for a dismal and shortened afternoon, and they were racketing through a narrow cut between some craggy and quite impressive mountains. To his surprise, David felt Janie's fingers weave in among his. He glanced at LaCoste, who averted his eyes and displayed a sudden interest in the workings of his reading light.

Several minutes went by before Janie said, "David, what if it is him?" and this time he had no inclination to correct her.

"That's just what I was thinking," he admitted. "If it is . . . look, baby, I think we'd better be careful. Approach with caution and all that."

She nodded as if she understood what he meant, although he was not at all sure himself. "The thing is, if he chose to die. And then years later he chose to come back to life at the same place. Well, he must have had a damned good reason, right?"

Janie nodded again, but for once seemed to have run out of words.

"Good enough so that he may not want anyone messing around, right? He might not welcome old friends, especially a busybody old friend from his previous incarnation, as it were."

"No, I see what you mean." To David's great relief Janie seemed impressed by what he said and subdued. Then with an unnerving flash of her normal mulishness she said, "But we have to find out. We can't just forget the whole thing and never know, can we?"

He supposed not, attractive as the idea was. "Whatever we do, though, let's not go crashing in. He doesn't have to know you're checking up on him. After all these years, he's not going to recognize you, is he? Unless you tell him"— David was abruptly, uncomfortably aware of LaCoste—"or someone else does."

Having conquered his reading light, the boy was bowed over his map. Now, feeling eyes on him, he looked up with a self-conscious smile.

"You're sure he doesn't understand English?" David said.

As if to prove this point, LaCoste tapped the window and pointed through it with pride. "El Ebro," he said. "El Ebro."

"It's a river," Janie said without bothering to look.

"I suppose it's no use asking him not to say anything to Luis," David decided. "About us, I mean. It would only call attention . . ."

"Luis Varga," Janie said. "It can't be."

Chapter 5

It was black-dark outside, a shiny wet night filled with confusing reflections, when they glided through the thickening lights of Bilbao and into the station. The train stopped with a clanking, lurching finality.

"Oomph." Pressed back into her seat, Janie showed no inclination to leave it, and David knew how she felt. LaCoste was gone. He had done the last miles hanging onto the brass rail in the corridor and with a hurried wave was first off the mark, as if he had a worthwhile date.

The compartment was snug and homelike while everything beyond struck David as problematical and requiring a great deal of coping, more than they were up to just then. There was no telephone here. As soon as they got into a hotel, they would have to call home. Would *want* to; David knew that he, too, would feel better when they had got through to Benny. Not that he was worried really, but Janie had introduced that grain of uncertainty. He only wanted to confirm that everything was all right. For several hours now—since lunch and the good red wine, he realized with a faint pinch of guilt—he had not given a thought to New York. The man, or men, called Luis Varga had provided such intriguing distraction, David could almost be grateful to him.

"Well, here goes," said Janie. It was the porter who forced matters, leading off through the corridor and, a fast length ahead of them, along the platform. Half into his raincoat, his arm jammed into the flapping sleeve, David would have liked a chance to look around. Above the gates and dwarfing them, there was a great luminous stained glass wall that reminded him of the huge Kodak panorama in Grand Central Station. Admirable hard-working figures seemed to represent the productive life of the region. David had a fleeting impression of fishermen straining over their oars before he hustled after Janie's distant figure and caught up with her at the taxi rank.

They had a choice of hotels, between the staid old Carlton where they had planned to stay and the new one that LaCoste had mentioned, out on the beach. Clearly it was the latter that drew Janie. "Because we did live out that way, and it's handy to the Old Port, if we're going to see Benny's father," she said, rationalizing a decision which David sensed had already been made, pending only some animated negotiations with the cab driver as to kilometers and pesetas. These established, David sat back as he would in a dentist's chair, with a fatalistic feeling that the rest was out of his hands.

The rainy streets shot past. Janie sat forward, braced against the back of the driver's seat, peering out anxiously at everything as if she might find a meaningful landmark.

"Yes, I do remember the river," she said at last, doubtfully, "and the boats, of course."

The brightly lighted boats and fiery mills cast their reflections across the oily water and high into the overhanging mist so that the riverfront was dramatically beautiful. Yet inhuman and somehow repellent, infernal, David thought, smelling the brackish river and tasting the yellow sulphurous smoke. And then he laughed aloud at himself for taking it so hard.

"Not exactly as advertised," he explained. "I was led to expect flounced petticoats and castanets."

"We'll see all that later. In the south," Janie said without turning. "After this . . ." vaguely.

His own malaise and depression and incipient headache were definite. It was the wine wearing off, he decided, a situation that he meant to remedy promptly at their hotel.

By the time they had registered and moved into their room, it was eight o'clock—a nothing time in Spain, David thought, if he could not reasonably expect dinner before ten. A nice time to make love maybe, or take a bath together, but stretched out on one of the beds he abandoned both ideas.

Janie had been prowling back and forth with one eye on her watch, unpacking, filling the time until she could call New York again. Now, fidgeting toward the phone, she perched on the bed beside him. "Maybe just a few more minutes, do you think?"

"Ummm." He probed the tiny knobs of her backbone. Having no idea how long it took to walk home from Aaron's school, he was for allowing them plenty of time. If Janie couldn't reach Benita this go round . . .

Incapable of sitting still, she swept aside the draperies and opened the door onto the balcony. A damp wind brought in the sound of a gently washing surf and the wet swish of an occasional car. For some time Janie stood worrying on the balcony, a shadow against the lights from the esplanade below, and then, panic in her voice, she said, "They must be there by now," and was jiggling the phone, signaling the switchboard.

"Señorita, por favor . . ." she began urgently.

That there was not to be an answer was evident after some twenty minutes of distorted Spanish and American and electronic sounds, of dialing again, allowing for human error or overworked circuits, of imagining the phones in their apartment, the one in the kitchen and the one in their bedroom, ringing on and on beyond any normal allowance in case Benita and Aaron were just coming in, and hurrying, hearing the ring, Benita was clumsy with the key.

"You know how fussed she gets. And emotional." Janie maintained a stranglehold on the receiver.

"Why not give up for now? Ask the operator to try again in an hour."

"Half an hour," she said.

They filled the time charting alternate routes home from Aaron's school. There were dozens of possibilities: not only the park and the market, but the ice cream parlor and the pet shop. It could take hours to drag Aaron past the pet shop, Janie said. Or Schwarz's. Somehow the image of Benny and Aaron hand in hand among the glories of F. A. O. Schwarz was reassuring.

At half-past nine she unpacked her address book. "Because if they're not home by this time—David, that's too long a day for a little boy—I'm going to call Dody Emmet."

"Good," he said tightly, displaying more strain than he intended.

Having failed and thwarted them repeatedly, the entire transatlantic system had begun to seem unworkable. As a result, when Janie asked for the Emmets' number, she was not at all prepared to have Dody's good strident New York accent come back at her within seconds. She stumbled over her explanations.

"No, no, there's no special message. It's just . . . well, if you could go over there, just to make sure everything's all right. I know . . . I mean, I'm sure it is, it's just that the phone's out of order or something, only . . ."

The question of Manolo's whereabouts was forgotten. Now Aaron was her only concern, and as she put this into words, distinctly, to enlist Dody's help, her fears became very real, very big.

David could hear enough to know that Dody had her own problems. Tomorrow, sure, but tonight . . . with three kids and Bud working late at the store on inventory, and even if she could get a sitter . . . Well, going out alone, after dark . . .

"Then tomorrow morning," Janie said. "First thing. And, Dody, listen, if Benny isn't there, could you wait for a few minutes. Get the doorman to let you in and you could check on the phone . . . and will you call me right back at this number, no matter what."

David took the phone from her as her throat constricted. "Dody, I think we'd better call you back. Same time tomorrow, okay? That ought to give you enough leeway. And, Dody, thanks.

"And now," he said when he had hung up, "we're going downstairs for a little food and a whole lot of wine."

But in the dining room an impeccably cooked *merluza* went unappreciated. "It's these crazy hours," David said, and refilled their wine glasses. "My patriotic stomach is still on New York time."

Her smile was polite but damp-edged. "Why on earth did we ever leave?"

"Why? Why, for fun and sun and romance, don't you remember? Our second honeymoon." A degree of sarcasm was warranted, he felt, but he should have left it at that. "Just the two of us off on our own, alone, free, dear lady . . ." He flung up his hands and knew instantly that he had knocked back a great deal of wine much too fast.

Janie had a frozen look. "You sound exactly like Nat Brandt," she said, and then slowly, as if a number of pieces were fitting themselves together, "Is that why? Was this all his idea, the trip, the whole thing?"

"But it's not what you think. I swear. Look, Janie, baby, will you listen to me? When I went to see Nat, I didn't think you were crazy. I just thought, frankly, you were making a big fuss about nothing, imagining things, whatever. All I knew was you were upset and things were getting pretty tense between us. That's why Nat thought a change might help, and I was all for a trip. Honestly, that's all there was to it. But I was afraid you'd misunderstand if you knew I'd consulted Nat. Damn it, I knew you'd take it the wrong way. You'd get mad and refuse."

"No, no, it's not that. It's just . . . I had the strangest thought. About Nat. About his prescribing this trip, sending us off to Spain. Can you remember how he put it exactly?"

"He said something about your recovering your youth. I guess he thought it was a good idea, getting you back here, if you've got some deep-seated hangup. Hell, I don't know. But you said yourself that things were coming back to you . . . repressed memories? If Nat's hoping to get at some unresolved problem, something left over from your childhood, I suppose this is a good place to start."

She had listened patiently. Now she shook her head with a look of regret. "I'm not talking about me. I'm talking about Nat himself. I know this sounds wild, but I suddenly thought there might be more to it. I thought maybe Nat had his own reasons for wanting us out of New York."

"But why? I don't get it."

Abruptly, as if she were pushing away the subject, she pushed away from the table.

"Janie, love. You really are letting your imagination run away with you," he said.

"Am I? Oh, David, I hope you're right. I hope that's all it is."

Chapter 6

By morning David devoutly wished himself back in New York, even back at the office. The known frustrations of the Digby account exerted an astonishing appeal.

He had spent the night with the surf and a harbor dredge pounding at him, aware that Janie was equally—but very separately—wakeful in the other bed. He had tried to see what she meant about Nat, but all he could see was Janie's troubled face as she had looked across the dinner table. Try as he would he could find nothing sinister in Nat's motivation, only in Janie's dark and worrying suspicions.

There it was again, the recurrent pattern that he had not wanted to take seriously, Janie imagining the worst, feeling spooked and threatened, seeing menacing figures everywhere: the man across the street in New York; the face in a painting, for God's sake, that reminded her of Manolo; and now it was Nat yet, sending them off to Spain for his own nefarious reasons! Or had Spain been Nat's idea? Sleepless at a disheartening half-past four, he was no longer sure of anything.

It was the telephoning that had upset them both, David reasoned, this business of not being able to reach Benita. They'd be fine after they'd heard from Dody Emmet. Certainly they would; it was lack of sleep that made him uneasy, that was all.

With first light Janie at last lay quietly, breathing evenly, and David slipped out of bed. The narrow balcony was icy under bare feet and wet still, as the chairs and table were, although the rain had stopped. He stood leaning against the railing and rubbing one foot, then the other, against the opposite leg for warmth.

With returning light the brownish tones of the sand and water emerged and on the far left, beyond the ruler-straight line of the breakwater, a blue rise of hills appeared not quite real but painted there for an illusion of depth. The Old Port, as Janie had described it, was on the right of the bay, nestled into the side of the cliff.

This was where Janie had lived as a child. When she was Aaron's age. Without notable success David tried to imagine the Vreelands here and Janie as she must have looked then, playing on this beach, watched over by Benita. But a young and pretty Benita then who was in love with a sailor called Luis. Luis Varga, who drowned. And now, somewhere along here—he leaned out as far as he dared, but could not get a clear view of the buildings that ringed the beach—somewhere nearby, there was a restaurant called Louie's Boat, El Barco de Luis, Luis Varga. It made no sense at all, except in the wayward illogic of a nightmare.

Bone-stiff with cold, he pushed back through the curtains, past Janie's bed, and ran a deep hot bath in the long Spanish tub.

At ten in the morning—twelve long hours before they were to call Dody; David confirmed this surreptitiously, his watch under the level of the table—Janie came down to the dining room. Her tweed suit, a gold and red and orange mixture like glowing autumn leaves, was too bright for her pale, drained face.

David had had breakfast and been across the street to the newspaper kiosk to pick up a London *Telegraph*. Now, keeping Janie company, he found that he was hungry again. Apparently it was true that misery not only loved company, it could make people fat. Out of frustration or worry, whatever their complaint, they overate. Being kind to themselves if the world was cruel? He toyed with this theory in silence while he poured out more of the milky coffee and piled a hard roll with butter and strawberry jam.

"It's awful having to wait all day. And half the night," Janie added with an undercurrent of blame.

"I know. I'm sorry, but with the time difference and all . . . Anyway, I thought it would be better not to have to hang around the hotel all day, glued to the phone."

"I suppose." She stirred her coffee for a full minute, staring out the window.

"Look familiar? The view, the bay," he specified when she seemed not to understand.

"Oh. No, not really. I didn't remember those hills at all, how close they are, the way they close in. I thought of the bay as much wider, undefined."

"You were much smaller."

"Yes . . ." She seemed dissatisfied. "And when the tide goes out, the beach will be quite a lot wider. But no, I don't identify with it, if that's what you mean. It doesn't all come rushing back. The lighthouse, for instance. Now that I see it, I know that it must have been there before, exactly where it is. But I wouldn't have remembered, if anyone had asked me . . . you know?" she finished with an air of giving up. There was something elusive, just out of reach, that obviously worried her.

"Now what time is it?" she asked a minute later.

"Ten twenty-two."

"They're not even awake yet in New York. Strange." And then, following this thought through, she said, "I must go see Benny's father."

"There's a pleasure I could live without."

"Then don't come."

"Don't be silly," he said quickly, and was not quite sure himself what he meant.

When they started out, the day had brightened to the extent that there was now a thin mustardy haze overhead. The air had a faint industrial flavor. "Just like home," David commented, "that nostalgic whiff of New Jersey."

Janie was not listening. Leading off along a paved walk that skirted the beach, she was searching the land side. Steep paths crisscrossed the grass and shrubbery here, approximating a green and brown Argyle pattern on the hillside. This part did ring bells. Rather to Janie's surprise, she suddenly remembered exactly how those paths had felt—coming down them, the slippery knee-jolting momentum; and the dragging, dry-throated climb at the end of an afternoon, Benita pushing and tugging, moodily if she had just kissed Luis good-bye.

"The things that must have gone on in those bushes!" She smiled briefly, recalling how she had been sent off to play.

But what she was looking for had not been there then. "It must be right along here," she said, hurrying on, and indeed, several new buildings later, it was.

El Barco de Luis was low, glass-fronted, rectangular— not at all boat-shaped. Outwardly, it was not yet awake. Nothing moved behind the plate glass, and the only sign of life was a single car, drawn up at the rear beside what was presumably the kitchen entrance. In an area of whitewashed or earth-toned buildings, Luis's restaurant had been painted an intense marine blue which the weather had streaked and faded.

"I take it that Louie's boat was blue."

David spoke facetiously and was not at all prepared for Janie's taut, "Yes, it was. Don't stare. Just keep on going."

He was only too willing to oblige. But he could not help turning, being drawn back to the unexceptional building. Whether it was the watery color, the washable blue ink shade, that reminded him, or the morbid pull that it some- how exerted, David found himself thinking of a tiny, evil Portuguese man-of-war he had once encountered on a Flor- ida beach. The inflated blue sac—he had thought at first that it was a plastic bag, tossed aside by a picnicker—had, once he had been warned away from it, held him spell- bound. It could not hurt him, all he had to do was walk away. Yet it had affected him as if the stinging tentacles could reach out through the sand. He had felt safer keeping an eye on the thing. He had had a feeling that it was watch- ing him.

He spoke lightly to cover his discomfort. "Then how do you propose to check out this character?"

She seemed to shake off the question. "I don't know exactly. It's all so unreal . . . being here like this." She put out her hand as if she needed to touch him—as she had on the train, he remembered—and this time he tucked her arm securely under his.

"There's something about this place, something I need to know about it, but I can't quite . . . it's as if I can't quite see, you know that feeling?"

He straightened his glasses in agreement but did not interrupt.

"But I feel as if I'm missing something important." She turned her head slowly, frowning at the beach and the bay.

"On the train," he prompted carefully, "you said all kinds of things were coming back to you, bit by bit."

"As I came back here, yes." She smiled quickly. "That's odd, isn't it, but that's how it was . . . as if I were moving back in time . . . finding things I'd forgotten."

"Luis Varga for one. You suddenly thought of his name. Do you remember what he looked like? Would you know him if you saw him?"

Janie nodded. "I wouldn't have. Two months ago, before we moved into my family's apartment, I'd have drawn a total blank. But there are photographs in Benny's room— old beat-up snapshots, they look as if she carried them in her pocket for years. There's one of her mother and father, taken some years before her mother died, but I'm sure I'll recognize old Don Pedro."

"And one of her beloved Luis?"

Janie smiled again. "Looking very young and hot-eyed

and sleek as an eel. He and Benny together and painfully self-conscious; it must have been when they were first engaged."

"Just before he drowned."

Janie's smile collapsed in confusion and something worse, a baffled kind of hurt. "Yes," she said. "It must have been."

The steps up into the Old Port did indeed suggest a journey back into a lost and long ago world. The steps themselves were crazily canted, eroded toward the center and worn slippery, like a rocky riverbed. Snugged together under loosely tiled roofs, meeting at unexpected angles, the houses presented an oddly united and impenetrable front as if they had quietly withstood wind and water and foreigners for several centuries. All were whitewashed, flaking, and as far as David could see through the small, random doors and windows, dark as caves.

It was a scene to delight a painter, he felt, but as a place to be paying a call, unlikely. "Now what?" he said.

"I ask."

Like the houses, the two black-bereted men she approached had a certain picturesque but inhospitable charm. Their deeply creased and weathered faces remained closed, distrustful of the question until they were quite sure that they understood it, and then, bobbing in unison, they bandied Don Pedro's name back and forth with frantic enthusiasm. What they were saying, in an all but incomprehensible accent that defeated Janie through several repetitions, was that Don Pedro would be at the tavern just down the way at this hour, he always was. With this they led the way, pointed through the low doorway to the first rough wooden table and stood back, still bobbing, with dignified curiosity.

Don Pedro sat alone, wrapped in the remains of a good gabardine raincoat. One big rough hand gripped a wine glass. At first glance in this dim place his rusty black beret, dashingly tilted over a strongly carved face, gave him the look of a much younger man. But his lower lids, seen closely, sagged away from his eyes, and he was slow to understand.

For a time he seemed incapable of speech except for repeating Benita's name, rather stupidly, after Jane. Then, very gradually, intelligence showed in his eyes, and his cracked lips widened. He said, "Chainee," once in a wondering tone, then over and over with growing warmth until her eyes filled with tears and she put her hand on his.

David decided that the only contribution he could make was a round of drinks, which he organized successfully by using a universal sort of sign language. That done, he sat patiently on the hard bench, resting on his elbows and guessing at what was being said. It was slow going obviously; their accents were too different and their common ground too tenuous. Even without the language barrier, David thought, his attention wandering, it would have been an all but impossible interview.

And then with a convulsion that threatened the table, the old man reared up on his elbows and spat succinctly on the floor. *"Manolo."*

A further string of expletives came out as an ominous growl and was followed by a long rumble of words, among which David caught only Chile, Argentina and New York. But that was enough; he had the gist. And if he hadn't, there was Janie's expression.

"Manolo hasn't been home for years," she said. "All that time, when I thought he was here, he was in South America, living it up . . . until lately, when he went to New York. Don Pedro has heard from Benita. She has been terribly upset, he says, terribly worried. David, why didn't she tell us!"

He could think of no answer. The old man, meanwhile, was shaking his head—letting it wobble back and forth—in an access of futility. "Ever since that time," he said, wearily now and speaking so slowly that Janie could translate as he went along, "when you were here. *That day!*" he said with a surge of excitement, his eyes glittering at Janie, expectant, and when she did not respond, he repeated angrily, "That day! Chainee, you remember . . . you were there!"

Incomprehensibly—and with a great effort, upsetting his bench—he got up. "I'll show you something. You come with me," he said.

David would have refused. He was rapidly being persuaded that Don Pedro was demented, or drunk, senile at best, and he put a hand on Janie's arm to stop her while the old man moved stiffly toward the door.

"It's all right," she said in a mesmerized voice.

"That's what you think," he grumbled, and there was no missing the childish ring of his words.

"He has something to show me, that's all. It seems terribly important to him. You could tell. Something happened . . . when I was here before, something big. He makes it sound like the biggest day of his life, and he's furious with me for not understanding."

"The day he won the fishing contest, no doubt, and he

wants you to see his prize catch. He's got it hanging on the wall."

She did not laugh. "Whatever it was, Manolo was involved, too. It had a bad effect on him, I gather."

"Janie, sweetie, the old boy is half off his rocker. He probably doesn't know what he's talking about either. It happens with age—hardening of the arteries, not quite enough blood to the brain, the memory gets spotty."

"Thanks a lot." She swung her legs over the bench and stood up. "Then it won't hurt to humor him. We'll make a good pair."

"Okay, maybe he's just lonely," David hedged, "and he's trying to hang onto you. Anything to keep the conversational ball rolling. But let's not get hung up on his trophies all day. Can't you just ask about Luis and have done with it?"

"You can stay here if you'd rather," Janie said from the doorway.

"Not on your life!"

"Then hadn't you better pay for the wine?"

Meekly, he offered the proprietor a handful of pesetas to choose from.

Janie and Don Pedro had gone on slowly, picking their way uphill over the cracked paving stones. If Don Pedro's feet were unsteady—and he did move with an elderly shuffle, feeling for the shape and stability of each footing—his hands and arms were vigorous. From the rear, as David watched, his sleeves and flapping coat took on a scarecrow vitality of their own. Arms outstretched, soaring, extended to a wingspan that as they swooped and dove threatened to topple his precarious balance altogether, he might almost have been a great ungainly bird. Or a boy being an airplane. And it was the latter, David realized, catching up, that the old coot sounded like, vibrating his mouth.

There was something grotesque about the performance, something imbecile, and about Janie's expression as she took it in with an unblinking, open-lipped fascination. The finale was painful to watch. Caught up in this travesty of flight, Don Pedro was completely above himself. He twirled once, dizzily, and dipped his great wings in a near-roll from which he barely recovered. Then, for several excruciating steps he ran, up on his toes, accelerating for a last roaring, plunging kamikaze dive.

But he was not quite through. Winded, panting and making worrying gasping sounds, he crouched against the wall of one of the houses, resting, waiting, and then with the most shocking suddenness, he exploded. His arms flailed over his head. Ferocious, inhuman sounds came out. And when at last mercifully it was over, there was a dreadful silence.

For a dazed moment David wondered if he should clap, if there should have been applause cards, if there would be a nervous titter from the audience.

"Good God," he said. Nobody seemed to hear him.

Don Pedro was adjusting his beret and eyeing Janie with a foxy kind of assurance. "You remember," he said, and walked on, signaling with a slight motion of his chin that they—or Janie, at least—should follow.

The approach to Don Pedro's room took them down a few steps below street level, past a door into the lower floor of the house, then sharp right up eight or ten more steps.

Don Pedro pushed on through the door ahead of Janie in his eagerness, and before David reached the top of the stairs, he reappeared in the doorway, holding whatever it was to the light.

Properly mounted or framed or suspended—and spotlit, say at the Whitney—the thing in his hands might have been labeled a found object, or even passed for sculpture. It was metal, and it had a twisted, tortured, blackened look. Without the old man's earlier performance, David might have had trouble guessing the significance of the thing. As it was, he was reasonably sure that it was a piece of an airplane that had come to a very bad end.

Janie clearly wanted no part of it. She kept her hands down and back, tensed at her sides, as if she might otherwise be forced to hold it, or accept it as a present. Don Pedro smiled at her—the stiff, cracked-lip smile that looked as if it must hurt—and shook his head. He was not about to part with this memento. He carried it back indoors and came back almost immediately bearing an even more puzzling artifact.

In this case the function was plain enough: it was a common, bladder-shaped type of wineskin, if a rather dusty and unsanitary one. David had seen them advertised as a flask for skiers, but its relevance here escaped him. He could not imagine that they were expected to drink from it.

To his immense relief, Don Pedro then pulled the plug and jounced the thing upside down as if to prove its emptiness. These actions were accompanied by a spate of intelligence so rapid and impassioned that David could not extract one word other than Manolo's name.

Janie, for her part, was only too obviously overwhelmed.

She could not possibly grasp everything the first time through, but bit by bit, hammered at by the old man's insistence that she remember—all but bludgeoned by his impatience as he, too, began to tire—she did understand him. David could almost have charted the progress of her comprehension by the rise of color through her neck and face into her eyes. She did not cry. She seemed parched instead, her mouth so dry that she could hardly talk at the end when Don Pedro pushed the wineskin at her.

Like a sordid prize won at a shooting gallery, it was still in her hand when they left.

Chapter 7

"Okay," David said. "What in hell was that all about?"

Now that they had come down out of the Old Port, it seemed possible to talk. And to breath again. He took in great gulps of the aromatic sea air as if he had been confined for too long among those treacherous and claustrophobic streets. Here, from the serpentine seawall, the bay and the beach looked wonderfully wide and open and modern and familiar. Odd how quickly it had improved, he thought, but this was no time to pursue the discovery. He and Janie had other subjects pressing.

"Do you want to tell me now?" Very gently he took the wineskin from her. The dark, hardened animal hide was unpleasant to touch. He threatened to get rid of it, to throw it as far away as he could over the seawall and into the water.

Janie stopped him. "Would you believe, that filthy thing was worth a fortune once?"

"No." He put it on the seawall. "Go on."

"I'm not sure I can explain. There are parts still . . ."

"I think you damned well better try. Now. You've been bottling things up too long, refusing to face them or talk about them . . ."

He had not meant to be tough with her, but he had to be. He had had enough of not understanding—not understanding the language or Janie, the fey and drifty evasions that, not understanding, he found frightening.

"So, out with it," he told her.

She looked startled. "You do sound like Nat Brandt," she said raggedly and then she was crying. She took a baby's iron grip on his lapels and burrowed into his shirt, sobbing and saying his name over and over again, at last wanting his help.

Like most cloudbursts, it was over as suddenly as it had started, but it left everything perceptibly changed. Janie unwound her fists and rubbed at her face, then pressed her palms against the top of the wall as if the gritty surface were astringent and steadying. She leaned on her hands as she talked, gazing out over the water with a certain wooden determination, like the figurehead on the prow of a ship facing into the wind. There was a small white sailboat playing in the bay between them and the lighthouse. Janie's eyes seemed to follow it. Without seeing it, David suspected.

"It was so awful at the end." She took one more deep breath to push down the last of her sobs.

"Then let's have it from the beginning."

"Yes, that's when it all started. That day, the day Don Pedro was talking about. I didn't know that he was there, too, but then he would have been. Everyone must have seen it."

"Seen what, baby?" he prompted when she showed signs

of drifting off into another silence. Her eyes moved the length of the beach now, searching it.

"There was a plane crash, wasn't there?"

She nodded. "Right there. On the beach. Up at the other end."

"And where were you?"

"Right there. Playing." She pointed to the near end of the sand. "Just at the edge of the water. We often came there. Or I did. Benita preferred the hill. You can see, there where the green starts. It was a lot more private for a rendezvous with Luis. So I spent a lot of time down there by myself, and that's where I was when the plane came down. It was unbelievable. Deafening. You can't imagine. The vibrations!"

"You must have been scared out of your wits."

"Oh, no. There wasn't time. And it was fabulous. It was the most exicting thing that had ever happened to me. You see, it came right in over my head and hit the beach and exploded, just like that, before I had time to think about it. And I saw the boy get away.

"That was the incredible part, how he was thrown clear—or jumped; I never did know how he managed it. But he did. I saw him slide underwater and then bob up again quite a way out, just about where that sailboat is now, so he looked like an ordinary swimmer. Then when everybody came racing to the scene—and did they ever! In minutes they'd swarmed all over the place. It was worse than a Sunday in the summer—he just climbed out on the breakwater over there and joined the crowd.

"I was absolutely fascinated, naturally. At first I thought he must be on fire or something when he went dashing into the water. Later I learned that he was a German soldier trying to escape. Spain being neutral, a lot of them tried to slip in that spring when they knew they'd lost the war. Anyway, this boy disappeared into the crowd. He was dripping wet and only wearing shorts.

"And Benita picked that moment to come and find me. I could have killed her. Really, cheerfully. With all this fabulous excitement on *my beach,* she was going to drag me away! You can imagine the state she was in, poor thing, and no wonder. She thought I'd been killed and it was all her fault for neglecting her little charge, lovemaking on duty or whatever. I can't believe she and Luis ever got very far in the circumstances—the Spaniards always were strict— but I'm sure she took this as a divine judgment on her sins."

Janie smiled wistfully. "It really must have been ghastly for her, and I was certainly no help. I'm told that I bit her. Anyway, I kicked and screamed and got away from her and vanished into the crowd myself. It was glorious."

David bit back questions. It was all he could do not to interrupt, but Janie apparently had to tell this her own way, from the very beginning—the good, happy part—or not at all.

"I found him again, the boy. I followed him. I don't know why. I suppose I was curious. And terribly overexcited about the whole thing. In a funny way, I think I felt quite possessive. He was my discovery. No one else seemed to know about him. Maybe because I was down so close to the water and he came out of the plane on that side . . .

"Anyway, so far as I know, nobody was looking for him. They found the pilot's body in the plane and that must have satisfied them. They didn't know there'd been a passenger.

Such a beautiful boy!"

Janie laughed. "Not a boy exactly. He must have been nineteen or twenty."

"Weren't you a little advanced for six?"

"Right on schedule, I should think. All set to play house with him." She looked very feminine at that moment, soft and merry, David couldn't help noticing, and he felt something amazingly like jealousy.

"And did you?" he asked.

"Oh, yes. It was bliss. You can't quite see from here," she said, trying, squinting at the hill, "and it may not be there any more, but near one of the paths, about halfway up, there was a funny little place. Sort of a little stone hut built right into the side of the hill, like a cave almost. I think they kept gardening tools in there. It doesn't matter, it was the kind of cubbyhole a child adores. And that's where my friend hid.

"I knew he must have, because he was on the path ahead of me, drifting away from the beach with the crowd, and then he wasn't, and I could guess where he'd gone.

"It was lovely. Like a game, knowing he was there. I wouldn't have given him away for anything. What I did do—and I have no idea how; I must have been a clever little sneak—was take him a blanket and a sweater of my father's."

"How very maternal."

"Yes, wasn't it!" Janie beamed. "Later I took him some more clothing, and food."

"I can see you now, like a busy little ant struggling along under enormous loads."

"It must have taken some doing to get past my mother

and Benita. But think of the fun it was to have a secret friend. A real one. You know how kids love secrets. They all do. I'm sure Aaron does . . . What do you suppose they are? David . . . ?"

She was no longer a naughty, delighted child. She took his wrist and turned it urgently, pushing back his sleeve to see his watch. "They'll be awake by now, won't they, in New York?"

"You'll have a full report in a few hours . . . in Dody's inimitable style. There's nothing to worry about," he added quickly. It was an empty assurance, meant only to undo this interruption.

"This secret friend of yours," he said, and laughed suddenly. "Did your father ever find out that he was provisioning the German army? Very embarrassing, I'd think, if anyone else found out . . . the American Consul!"

"I don't know." Janie looked bewildered.

"You couldn't have kept him a secret forever."

"Oh, no. Manolo saw to that. Naturally. I wonder what Brock would have done. If he'd been left alone, I mean. I wonder if he had a plan." She spoke in a halting, tentative way as if her fragmented memories of that time were bits of a puzzle, and some of the pieces might have been irretrievably lost.

"Brock was the German?"

"It's what I called him. His name sounded something like that. We had our own makeshift language, as I remember, very limited—he knew a few words of English—and we used a lot of sign language, which was fine but basic. Very basic." She smiled. "Not up to abstract things like plans."

68

"He didn't try anything, any funny business, I mean. On you."

The prudish, shocked sound of this made her laugh out loud, but she seemed gratified, too. "Good Lord, no. I'd have screamed bloody murder and run a mile. At that age. No, if anything he came down to my level. And the wineskin"—she looked at it there, ugly on top of the wall—"was a toy. A bag of marbles. That's just what it was like. Full of bits of glass. That's what I thought they were at first, glass beads, and I thought it was a little odd of him, but very nice that he cared so much about them. At his age."

David raised an eyebrow, sharing this view.

"They were diamonds, of course. Most of them. A few rubies, and I think some sapphires, and an emerald or two."

"Good Lord." He reconsidered the wineskin. It looked no better, but now merited a horrified respect. "Some toy," he said.

"And we played with them. We really did. It was wild . . . fantastic. That's how it must have seemed to him: unreal, like winning the Irish Sweepstakes or something. He couldn't believe his luck. The whole lot, handfuls of them, had been collected by his commanding officer, who was some high mucky-muck. Illegally, you can bet, and I hate to think how he got his hands on them. But he did, and they were to save his neck. And then he died in the crash. He was the pilot. And Brock was left holding the wineskin, literally; he'd been ordered to hang onto it for dear life, I gather, and there it was in his hands when they crashed. He knew what was in it, and his first thought was to hide it somewhere. I suppose in case he was picked up. Anyway, that's what he was doing swimming out in the bay. He wasn't on fire. He was hiding the wineskin. You see over there?"

She pointed to the long stone jetty that bisected the bay. "You can almost see. About halfway along there are steps down into the water. It's a sort of landing place for boats, whether the water's high or low."

"Clever," David said absently. There was something nagging at him—something just beyond the reach of his memory.

"Brock had found a hole where some rocks had fallen out. He'd wedged the wineskin into it. It was a wonderful hiding place. I think they'd have been safe there forever, if he hadn't taken them out himself. To play with," she marveled, "and he gave me some."

David half heard. Half his mind was groping back through what Janie had been saying, searching for whatever it was that had almost reminded him of something.

"I think he gave me an emerald and some diamonds. I'm not sure. I lost them," Janie said. "I was probably careless —I was so young, I had no idea of their value—but I always wondered, I suspected Manolo. Because he knew. He was always following me, spying on me."

Janie's anger was quick and vivid as a child's. Her face was flushed and tough with resentment, as if at some very recent offense. "He spoiled everything. He made Brock run away. It was his fault. Everything . . ."

The shrill, unnatural voice grated and became faintly repellent, like a bad impersonation. David listened with growing horror, feeling Janie slip away, back into another time, another self.

And at the same moment he knew what it was that had been eluding him.

All along here, constantly lapped at and left slimy by the tides, the stepped boat landings disappeared into the murky water. Leaning over the wall, he could see one just below them at the side of a stubby cement pier. The bottomless stone stairway went down into the water evenly and steadily, like a deliberate drowning. The effect was disorienting—David thought of whole houses awash in flood waters; there was something unsettling, uncanny about it.

"Steps going nowhere," he said aloud, tentatively.

Janie's expression was illegible. Opaque at first, uncomprehending, touched with irritation as if he had interrupted her with inanities. Then grateful, as if he had shown astonishing perception.

"Yes. Exactly," she said. "That's where it happened. Oh, David." Unaccountably, she clutched at him again and huddled against him.

It was a long time before she spoke again. She kept her eyes tightly closed—every muscle in her body felt tensed and resistant—and David could only hold her and wait out her despair.

"God damn Manolo," she said at last, choking on the rage that had been held back too long. "I never would have killed anybody. I couldn't have! If only . . ."

She pounded on David with frustrated fists.

Chapter 8

"It wasn't enough that he spied on us," Janie said when he had immobilized her wrists and, holding her close against him, finally steadied her.

"He had to tell on us, too. He told Benita. And she of course told Luis. Otherwise . . . Oh, David, if they'd only left us alone. If Luis had only stayed out of it."

She took a ratchety, difficult breath. "He would have been all right. He wouldn't have died. He would have married Benny and lived happily . . ." She foundered on a breathy sob.

David tightened his grip as if he could keep her from slipping away, back into that shadowy, terrifying time. As if he had to keep her awake in order to keep her out of her very private and incommunicable nightmare. He found himself forming wordless prayers. What would Nat Brandt do now? Faced with this unnerving double-think, this divided, warring memory of Janie's, would Nat try to reason with her, to comfort her, or simply let her run on while he listened judiciously? Janie, he answered himself, was not Nat's wife.

He smoothed her hair. "Janie, baby, listen. Luis may not be dead, remember? You told me yourself. There's a Luis Varga who has a restaurant here. Louie's Boat, remember? Right over there."

She shook her head, shaking away his hand. "That's what I wanted to think. But it's not true. I know. I was there, David. I saw the whole thing. I *should* know. *I killed him!*"

Nat Brandt would never have panicked and shaken Janie in anger—David knew that with a strange certainty, even as he did it—until her head wobbled on her neck like a doll's on a broken elastic. Appalled, he realized when it was over that he would have done almost anything to stop the hysterical outburst.

And then, feeling sick, he pressed his hand over her mouth very gently and said, "Shut up, baby. You never killed anyone in your life. You couldn't if you had to."

Her eyes were closed, not so much to shut out disturbing images as to shut them in, like slides projected in a darkened room, where she could see them more sharply. Her lips moved under his palm.

"I did," she mumbled. "I killed him."

He pressed harder until she caught the fleshy base of his thumb between her teeth and bit into it.

"When Brock was trying to get away," she said, "I didn't want to remember all that. I tried not to . . . for such a long time."

Helplessly David stroked her.

She opened her eyes and blinked once or twice at the yellow glare, then stared straight ahead across the water toward the steps at the side of the long stone jetty.

"Brock was in a boat, a rowboat," she said softly, reconstructing the scene bit by bit. "It was a misty night, almost dark. He'd gone to get the wineskin. We'd put it back for safekeeping after we were sure that Manolo had seen it. I don't know why I was there. I shouldn't have been. To say good-bye, I suppose. And Manolo and Luis followed me."

Remembering, forcing herself to remember and to talk about this, she looked stunned and lost, and her words had a flannelly dry sound. "It was so awful," she said. "The three of them like animals, clawing and charging at each other.

"Brock in his boat. I think he'd already got the wineskin. Yes, I know he had. I remember his hands scraping on the rocks, trying to hold the boat alongside, and scrabbling in the wall, hurrying, because he could see Manolo and Luis coming, running toward him down the pier. He had the wineskin, all right, but he hadn't got very far, not far enough. He had only just pushed off and Manolo made a flying leap—right into the boat on top of him.

"And then Luis started . . ." Janie hesitated, seemingly overwhelmed by the confusion and shock of that moment, and when she went on it was in a flat, dead tone. "I'll never know what happened. Not for sure, will I?"

It was such a desolate question, David longed to give her a comforting answer, but there was none.

"Whether I meant to do it. All I know is he started past me, running, ready to dive . . . and I wanted to stop him. And then, I don't know . . . whether I tripped him. Anyway he lost his balance. He hit the steps. And broke his neck or fractured his skull. What difference does it make?"

she said with a sudden, desperate carelessness. "Or if he just plain drowned? It all happened so fast. He was running . . . and then he looked so strange, sinking into the water. I wonder if he could have been saved.

"The other two, Brock and Manolo, were fighting over the wineskin. I remember the boat rocking wildly and the oars flopping and banging. I don't think they were aware of anything until it was too late. I don't know if I said anything, if I shouted at them. I don't think I did. I think it was like one of those dreams. That's how I remember it. I couldn't make a sound. But I could run, and that's what I did. I ran home. And I never said a word about it to anyone. Until now."

For quite a long time David simply held her, pitying her, thinking of that terrified, lonely little girl bottling up her unspeakable guilt. Then with one arm lightly around her he guided her away from the seawall, leaving the wineskin there where he had put it. If Janie noticed it, she did not object.

When they had gone some distance back toward their hotel, David said, "Then you don't *know* that he died. If you left, you can't be absolutely certain."

"Oh, it was definite enough. They recovered his body. There was a funeral."

"Did you ever think someone else might have killed him? After you left, I mean?"

She smiled miserably. "It would be nice, wouldn't it? I'd like to think that he bobbed up again, like magic, and Manolo turned on him. Or Brock even, in self-defense, but . . ." Her hands moved in a weak, empty gesture.

"Poor baby."

"I never saw Brock again. He got away. That was the one good thing."

"With the jewels?"

"I thought so. At least that's what I assumed at the time. They were the least of my worries. But I thought he'd got off with them, to South America or somewhere," she said vaguely, as if her attention had been caught by something else, another piece of the puzzle that just might fit.

"Now I see," she continued. "It was Manolo. I should have known. He said an odd thing afterwards. He said he wouldn't tell on me. He said he'd never tell anyone what I'd done if I promised not to talk about it to anyone, ever. It was an easy enough promise to make, you can imagine.

"He said that no one need know that I'd had anything to do with Luis's death—it could be passed off as an accident, an accidental drowning—and it would be better, in fact, if I hadn't been there at all. So he would leave me out of it altogether if I solemnly promised, cross my heart and hope to die, that I'd forget the whole thing. If I'd forget that I was even there . . .

"I thought it was awfully nice of him, surprisingly. It wasn't a bit like him to be kind. It didn't occur to me that he was only protecting himself. Of course, I can see that now, looking back. If he had the jewels, he certainly didn't want a major investigation. This way, he had it made: Luis dead and out of the way; me silenced for life, afraid to peep; and Brock obviously in no position to complain. All very nice and tidy."

"And Benita?" David asked.

"She was so broken up about Luis, I don't imagine she could think about anything else. Anyway, she probably didn't know about the jewels. I doubt that Manolo mentioned them."

The effort of reconstructing that time, of facing it and telling David about it, had left Janie exhausted, yet visibly relieved. For a moment, as if a long-known pain had eased at last, her taut face cleared. It was a brief remission.

"All very nice and tidy *for him*," David mimicked furiously. "Sure. Peachy. He walks off with the prize and leaves you with a lifetime supply of guilt! Afraid to think even. It doesn't take a psychiatrist to see what he did to you. Talk about blackmail . . ."

"But it's all right, David. I'm all right now, don't you see? Now that I've told you . . ." She trailed off doubtfully. Then, "David, what did you mean? About blackmail? If Manolo is in New York. With Benny. And Aaron . . . ?"

"There's nothing to worry about. He won't hurt Aaron."

"I've got to know. I can't stand waiting any longer. What time is it?"

It was seven minutes past three. "They'll have finished breakfast at home," David said. "Dody will be on her way over to the apartment any time now."

"What will we do?"

"Wait," he said, and then callously, because his own fear made it necessary to be tough: "Have lunch. It will kill some time. How about El Barco de Luis?"

Chapter 9

Ten o'clock in the morning is a good time to go crosstown in New York, as good a time as any, Dody Emmet decided. With her five-year-old mercifully doing his incessant thing at nursery school, she had only ages two and four to contend with, Jamie and Meg, one hand for each. So that she could have managed by bus, but at the last rationalized herself into a taxi instead.

For one thing, it was cold out. The easy Indian summer weather was suddenly gone, and a blustery wind carried premonitions of rain and winter. And she was running late, by the time she had assembled two pairs of mittens. Then Meg, in an inconvenient fit of vanity, chose—no, demanded, as effectively as any striking union—her new winter coat, which still needed extensive shortening. Dwarfed by it as she was now, she would be no credit to her mother on the upper East Side.

Nor had Don's opinion helped, his saying at breakfast that it was all nonsense, and now that she thought of it, she wondered what he had meant exactly. Janie's worrying so much, was that what he found senseless? Or her going all the way over there to check on the apartment?

"Just give their number another try, why don't you? Benny's pretty sure to be there this time of day." Easy enough for him to talk and then take off for the store and nothing to worry about but sports and games, like a big overgrown kid with his smooth round face and his bicycles and baseball equipment, and skis now.

But Benny did not answer. Dody let the phone ring on and on—it sounded normal enough to her—and she imagined it sounding through the empty apartment, over and over, and wondered if the useless ringing was beginning to annoy the neighbors and decided not; the walls there would be thick and good, properly built.

It was not as if Dody wanted to go over there. She found Benita dauntingly foreign under the best of circumstances, and she was not sure how she would explain this intrusion, this checking up critically as it might appear through the fuzzy signals of their two languages. This problem occupied her during the crosstown ride so that she was curt with the children while rehearsing the most diplomatic of speeches in basic English for the Spanish woman's benefit. As a result, she arrived feeling fussed—the careful speeches would, she knew, come out nervously backwards—and then there she was pouring out her troubles to the doorman, garrulously losing face.

". . . I mean, I don't want her to think I'm snooping or anything like that. It's just that, being so far away and all and not getting any answer, naturally Mrs. Ingstrom was worried, and she wanted me to see about the phone, really that's all it is, make sure it's working, you know?"

For his part the doorman remained warily cool. He maintained in fact the general look of a man whose bunions were aggravated by the weather. All he conceded was that he could take her up in the elevator all right, if that was what she had in mind, but he couldn't guarantee it would do her any good.

"Could be I'm wrong," he said without conviction. "There's some that comes and goes without my seeing them, I can't be everywhere at once and there's nothing to stop them using the stairs, but it must be two or three days now —at least that, maybe more—I haven't seen either one of them, the maid or the boy."

The wormy feeling in her stomach was from the elevator, that's all it was. From the old-fashioned lurching rise, Dody told herself. She took a firm grip on Jamie's mittened hand and on Meg's dangling cuff.

The doorman waited in the elevator with the door propped open and a distant buzzer going unanswered while she saw for herself. The doorbell rang clearly enough. She could hear it shrilling through the apartment so that no one could help hearing it, but there was no answering motion at all.

"Then you'll have to let me in. You have a key, don't you?" she said coldly.

He eyed the children, apparently not as proof of her reliability but as a threat to the premises. At this impasse, Dody supposed, the worldly thing would have been a crisp new bill crackling between them. She visualized the tarnished change in her purse and the ten dollar bill that was her last, and sternly addressed the children.

"You will keep your hands behind your back and touch

nothing," she said, "while Mummy tries the telephone and writes a note to Benita. Since we've come this far, and I've got to have something to tell the Ingstroms when they call back tonight, all the way from Spain . . ."

Again the doorman held the door propped open and himself expressly detached, wrapped in negative opinions. To Dody's surprise, the children, too, held back and remained rather worryingly well behaved in the outer hallway.

There *was* something off-putting about the Ingstroms' apartment. What Dody remembered as a bright and enviable living room looked gray now in the light that filtered between half-drawn draperies—and depressingly tidy, like a hotel room on an air shaft. She had an impulse to push back the curtains and throw open windows. That was the worst of it, the lifeless air and the old odors, disagreeably compressed. She had an overriding wish to finish her business and leave.

The lively dial tone startled her—she had somehow expected less—and she dialed Don's store with a jerky kind of urgency as if her hands were nervous.

"Don, listen. It's me. I'm here at the Ingstroms'. No, Benny isn't here, and I'm not going to wait. I'll leave her a note and tell her to call me. But try this number, will you? I just want to make sure."

There was no problem. She had hardly put down the receiver when the bell rang under her hand. "Right. Well, that's fine then. I'll see you tonight, hon," she said, and added, "Don . . . ?" suddenly wanting to hang onto him, to say something more, she was not sure what. But he had hung up already, and he would think she had flipped if she called back now.

She found a pencil and a grocery list pad in the kitchen and left her note for Benita there, carefully printed in big legible letters. Then, only because something more seemed called for, she went through the rest of the apartment, hurriedly and with none of her usual interest. Benita's room, Aaron's, Janie's and David's: everywhere the same terrible tidiness, and in the hall that nasty smell.

"All right," she said, and the doorman released the door so that it closed loudly behind her, but she stood there for a moment, dissatisfied still, trying the doorknob, double checking. "The telephone is working all right."

He nodded with a silent sarcasm that all but goaded her into showing him her empty hands and the innocent contents of her pocketbook. "Tell Benita to call me the minute she comes in," she said.

It was then that the stress of good behavior began to tell on the children. "I want to play with Aaron," Jamie announced.

"Where's Aaron? We want to play with Aaron," Meg took up the cry with a whine that flicked Dody's nerve endings.

"Don't be silly. He's at school," she said. "At this hour . . ." Of course he was in school, she repeated to herself firmly. It was just odd—but not impossible, she argued, with a full-time maid like Benita—that there wasn't the slightest sign of a little boy anywhere in that apartment, no socks on the floor or rumpled pajamas, not so much as a cereal flake crunching underfoot.

Originally she had thought that, as long as they were over here, they would go on to Bloomingdale's, maybe stop for a treat at Schrafft's. Now, abruptly, all she wanted to do was go home. She pushed the children into a taxi. She wanted to go home and call Aaron's school. She had to be sure.

They were cutting through the park when she thought about the smell in the hall. She could almost taste it still, caught high up at the back of her throat. Incongruously it was mixed in her mind with perfume and flowers and white frosted cake, all the sweet fragrance of a wedding, her cousin's wedding. The reception had been held at home, and Dody clearly remembered the creeping suspicion, the tracing and sniffing, the appalled denials, and the ultimate whispered certainty that there was something dead in the wall.

Chapter 10

"Funny," David confessed with the slight smile that the word required, "this place gave me the creeps a while ago. It reminded me of a Portuguese man-of-war."

"And now?" Janie asked. She had come to a stop, with an air of balking, in front of El Barco de Luis.

The admission of his earlier cowardice had a strengthening effect, that combined with Janie's reluctance. "Now I'm starved," he said, but as the mention of food clearly turned Janie off, he added more tactfully, "and curious, frankly, now that you've filled me in on Luis."

"It's a common name, a coincidence, that's all."

"Oh? You didn't think so before. And what about the girl he left behind, the one he came back looking for, or whatever it was?"

"Spaniards love romantic stories," she said.

"Just have a glass of wine then. Come on."

"I couldn't. Not now, David. I couldn't possibly."

He could not have said why all of a sudden he was so determinedly on the other side. It could have been Janie's remote and private way of suffering, her way of shutting him out. Or the time, the intolerable waiting before they could be sure that everything was all right at home. All he knew was that at this juncture almost any action would be better than none.

"What have you got to lose?" he said, and in a softer tone, "Look, Janie. If by any chance it is Luis, your Luis . . ."

"He's dead. I told you." She turned her back and would have walked away, but he caught her wrist.

"Don't you see, sweetie, You'd be off the hook altogether, clear conscience."

"You go," she said. But it was not, as he first thought, an abrupt brush-off; she was pleading with him. "Please, David, you go in and find out. I'll go on ahead. I'll wait for you by the breakwater."

"But I wouldn't recognize him if I saw him. I wouldn't know him from Adam."

"Yes, you would. By his hand. I don't remember which one, but Luis was missing the ends of three fingers. It's the sort of thing that fascinates kids. It's what I remember best about him, those three stubby fingers. David, thank you," she said, settling the matter with such gratitude that he could hardly refuse. This time he let her go.

The restaurant was definitely, as the young man from the telephone company had said, humble. There was a single plain room, devoid of any nautical touches except for a certain fishy pungency and a view of the bay.

David chose a table by the window and sat so that he faced in the direction of the breakwater. He could see Janie from here, her meandering, time-killing progress. Receding along the promenade, dwarfed by the wide arc of the beach and the bay, she seemed reduced to Aaron's size—and equally defenseless. He felt the same sharp protective tug that he had felt when watching Aaron from a distance.

Inside the restaurant there was a cheerful gabble of late lunchers, several tables of them passing pitchers of wine around or, with infinite time and patience, probing miniature snail-like shells, coaxing out the tiny bodies on the tips of straight pins. David looked further for something more substantial and less demanding in the way of nourishment and in the end, by inelegantly pointing, succeeded in ordering wine and grilled fish.

He could give his full attention then to the question of the owner's identity. In New York, he supposed, he would simply have asked. But here? Even if he had had full command of the language, he thought that he would have been reticent here. Discreet perhaps was a better word. There was too much that he did not understand. Whether it was Janie's experience—and that painful revival of a terrible childhood trauma—or the place itself, the alien smell of it and the foreign faces, he was unsure of himself, uneasy and a long way beyond his usual depth.

For a moment he had lost sight of Janie—she must have blended against the wall there where the promenade joined the breakwater—and now he saw her again starting out along the top of the breakwater. He was sure that it was she; her bright outfit and her fair hair were unmistakable.

By his hands, Janie had said. He would know *the* Luis by his hands, which at a glance eliminated the two waiters, both of whom had a full complement of fingertips.

Along the inner wall of the restaurant there was a bar

where two men, half hitched onto tall stools, were having coffee and cognac and a roaring dispute with the bartender. Judging by the pounding of their fists and bellows of derisive laughter, they were replaying an especially hard-lost game. Football, David guessed from the few words he understood. He was intent on their hands, waiting for the man behind the bar to show his. Stocky, muscular, with thick, scowling eyebrows; he looked about the right age.

At home David could have gone over to the bar, eased into the conversation, or at least, needing a pretext for a closer look, he could have ordered a drink or reached for a toothpick. Here . . .

The man behind the bar reacted to being stared it. "You want something, mister?" His tone was not exactly that of a bartender taking an order, and his eyebrows had drawn together in a challenging line.

Jolted, David did not at first notice that the words were English, and then in a fumbling sort of double take he blurted. "No, thanks. I mean, yes. I was looking for someone. I was wondering. Are you by any chance Luis?"

The man needed a few seconds to sort this out. When he had, he jabbed at his chest and snorted and by a backward stretching of the neck indicated that Luis would be in the kitchen. Continuing this line of inquiry, however, by stepping to the doorway and actually looking, he corrected himself. "Was here," he said, puzzled. "You wait."

There was a pause during which David's fish and wine arrived and the barman found further English words. "When you finish to eat," he promised, "Luis here."

His two buddies nodded, agreeing. They had pivoted to study David during this exchange, and now they continued to observe him as if interested in his opinion of the fish, which was good, and the sour wine.

Janie, meanwhile, had advanced some distance along the breakwater. Sauntering, stopping now and then, she was nearly halfway out, approaching the landing steps, very close to the place where the jewels had been hidden. That god-awful place where it all happened, David thought, and all at once wondered why on earth she had gone there, how it would be for her, if she was all right, alone there. He should have stayed with her. He should never have let her go on alone.

To the distress of his audience, he put down his fork. He could no longer taste the fish, anxiety had so constricted his throat. He found himself squinting, his strained eyes resenting the distance and the window.

As if she, too, needed to see more clearly, she bent over as he watched her, then knelt and reached over the edge and ran her hand along the rough stones. For a moment David doubted his own senses. He resisted what he saw as too eerie, unreal, Janie deliberately moving through what he could only think was a reenactment of the tragedy, for now she was on her feet again, walking to the stairs, starting down them. . . .

Her head came up with a snap. She stood absolutely still for a moment in a listening attitude, immobilized on the third step.

David could only guess at what had stopped her. There were other people, a scattering of other walkers along the breakwater. One of them, he thought, must have warned her off the steps. In any case, to his intense relief, she climbed back to the top and went on, briskly now toward the lighthouse at the far end.

Until then it had not occurred to David that someone was following her. But now one of the other figures was walking faster, too. Out of the random pattern of late afternoon strollers on the pier, one had detached himself and was moving as Janie did, walking rapidly, then more rapidly and at last breaking into a run.

Something crashed to the floor as David pushed away from the table. He did not stop to see what it was but went hurtling out of the door, aware of protests behind him, the bartender shouting what sounded like, "Hey, you pay!" but he did not stop for that either. What mattered was getting to Janie.

While he had been looking for Luis—heroically sitting there waiting for him, eating and drinking, for God's sake— Janie had found him all right . . . and she was running for her life.

His own feet pounded harder on the pavement, his heart hammering and a stitch catching at his side. The promenade stretched endlessly ahead.

When he had rounded onto the breakwater itself, he could no longer see Janie. Other people intervened, and it was all he could do to dodge between them and keep his footing on the broken surface. When at last he was forced to stop, aching and shuddering for breath—and by then he was past the fatal steps and had a clear view to the end of the breakwater—Janie was gone.

There was no one between him and the lighthouse, only the shockingly empty dun-colored expanse.

She had to be there somewhere. Unless he was losing all his marbles, she was around behind the lighthouse. And so was Luis.

With this thought he was running again, propelled by a surge of panic, to the very tip of the jetty. But here, too, on the far side of the lighthouse, he found an unbelievable emptiness. There was nobody at all, nothing but the racketing of his own pulse and as that at last subsided the sound of the water licking at the pier. Rough, unfathomable water here in the channel and Janie . . .

He could not control the images that flashed through his mind . . . of Janie floating limply beneath the surface, trapped and held down by the weight of her water-logged clothing. The heavy wool suit, the glowing colors. David's eyes swept back and forth over the water, aching to see deeper, dreading a bright orangey glint. He squeezed his eyes tight shut to rest them, and opening them tried to sharpen his focus by staring across the channel.

He was not sure what caught his attention, whether it was a sound or a motion somewhere behind him. He only knew that he sensed someone and he turned quickly, braced and sharply conscious of his own exposed position. At first he saw no one and then, as he crept around the curved base of the light, he looked down on a lower walkway. Another stone stairway joined the two levels and further stone steps continued steadily down into the sea, their worn surfaces left green and slimy by the receding tide.

They were on the lower steps, the man crouched over Janie, hiding her face. What David could see was that her suit was dark wet and, sagging under its own weight, dragged against her body. Then the man straightened, lifted Janie and held her closely.

"You bastard!" David did not stop to think. He hurdled

the first steps as he shouted, "God damn you, let go of her. Leave her alone, you . . ."

He did not let go, but his head came up, startled, and David saw Janie's face, the wide-open eyes and dripping, flattened hair.

"David!" Her voice, too, sounded drowned. "Be careful, it's . . ." Shivering, chattering, she struggled with the words. "It's slippery."

"Janie . . . oh, God. Are you all right?"

"Yes. Yes, I think so. Now. I mean, it's Brock. David, it's Brock."

The man nodded, his broad-boned face stern, and said, "She is very cold." He released Janie then to shrug out of his coat.

"Oh, no, you don't." David peeled off his own jacket and, pulling Janie to the top of the steps, wrapped her in it.

"I'm all right, darling. Really," she insisted, but he could feel her shaking. Giggling and sobbing, she did her best to complete the introductions. "He's Brock. My German friend, remember? Brock, this is David. My husband. David, Brock is Luis, Luis is Brock!"

Brock raised a hand to quiet her. "Forgive me," he said. "Please. I am sorry for everything." He turned to David then with a stiff smile. "I did not mean to frighten her so much. Only to see if it was Jane, if it was possible after so many years, when she went by . . ."

"And you recognized her, just like that," David interrupted, "when you hadn't seen her since she was a little girl. Come off it!"

"I could only hope, from what one of my customers told me, about the American señora on the train who had lived here as a child."

"My friend from the telephone company."

"Christ. I should have known! Even then," David's anger swelled, "did you have to scare her to death, chasing her that way?"

"Please, I only wanted to explain."

"It was my fault for running." Janie was trembling still, but regaining control. "I don't know what got into me, why I panicked so, only . . .

"I had been reliving it all. Everything came back to me so clearly, so overwhelmingly: the feel of the pier and the smell of the water, the way everything looked from out here. And Luis. I'd been thinking so hard about Luis, trying to remember exactly . . .

"So that when I thought I heard someone say my name, he was the first person I thought of. The only one. I went on then, to see if someone really was following me, and he was! And all I could think of was getting away. But I couldn't run forever."

Janie was breathless again, remembering. "So when he was behind the lighthouse and couldn't see me, just for a minute, I ducked down these steps. To hide, until he went past. I didn't know they were so slippery." She shivered again.

"But you are too cold now. You are freezing. We will talk later," Brock said.

Chapter 11

"Now," they said in a ragged near-unison that made Janie laugh again, her composure uncertain even after a long hot shower and a change of clothing. Brock, worrying over her and taking command to a degree that David found excessive, had refused to give another word of explanation until Janie was dry.

For privacy they had chosen to have drinks in the Ingstroms' hotel room. There was a bottle of Scotch and a bucket of ice on the dressing table at David's elbow. Janie, cuddling her drink, was curled against a pile of pillows on one of the beds, smug as a cat and all but purring. She could hardly take her eyes off Brock.

"I can't believe it. It's so good . . . I'm so glad," she said at intervals and then, lacking adequate words, she merely smiled her contentment.

Brock sat in the comfortable chair by the balcony doors, which were closed now against the cool evening, so that the bay was shut out and silenced.

"Now," Brock said. "I will tell you what happened."

David hunched forward on the dressing table bench and Janie went totally still.

"As I told you, I assumed Luis's identity. I became Luis, on his boat, everywhere. It was strange that, how it worked out."

"Then Luis is definitely dead? At the risk of sounding stupid," David said, "he did die that day?"

"But you knew that, surely?"

Brock looked to Janie, who nodded. "But I thought there might be some mistake. When I heard he was here, running a restaurant, I thought maybe, and then out on the pier, when you called to me and I thought it was Luis after me." She abandoned that sentence and started again. "You see, all this time, I didn't let myself think about him, because I thought I'd killed him."

"You! But you were a child, a tiny little girl. You couldn't have killed a bumblebee!"

"Manolo said . . ."

"Manolo." He spit out the name. "Of course. He would. Janie, you were not there even. I saw you run away, like a little rabbit."

"Afterward. I ran away after I tripped Luis, or pushed him . . ."

Brock made a derisive German sound. "You couldn't know. You couldn't see what happened after you left. But I can tell you, Luis was not dead. He was much alive, you can believe me, when he swam to my boat. The two of them, Luis and Manolo, took away the jewels. Which one had them first, that I could not say. It was all I could do to save myself."

Brock's smile was sad and remote, that of a man looking

back a long way. "They fought it out on the pier, and I assure you, Janie, you did not cause Luis's death."

"Manolo did?" she said.

"There is no doubt. I could see plainly. And then I, too, must run, not to be implicated. You understand?" He looked from Janie to David and, satisfied, went on.

"In those times, you must remember, when there was so much killing, the living took from the dead. To survive. I had seen that. That must be why I went to his boat. To take the place of the dead man." Again he looked to each of them for understanding and accepted Janie's puzzled nod.

"His papers. His job. His berth. It was my escape. On the boat, they care only that the work is done, and I went quickly to another boat. And another, all around the world. Always I am Luis Varga."

He broke off and stared with delight at Janie. "Always I hope to see you. To thank you," he said.

"To thank *me!*" The words caught, and she cleared her throat before she tried to speak again. "Do you realize what you've just done for me? Do you have any idea how it was, that awful guilt . . . and now to be free of it? To know for sure, not to have that worry any more."

"You have no worry," Brock said.

The words hung in the air for a moment like a benediction. David stood up gratefully to replenish their glasses, with a sense of occasion, as if a toast might be proposed.

Janie came upright with a jerk that splashed Scotch onto the bedspread, saying, "Oh, God. What time is it?"

Chapter 12

They put the call to Dody Emmet in early. "She'll be back. She'll be home for the kids' lunch," Janie insisted. "I know."

David was easily persuaded. The call went through at half-past twelve, New York time, and Dody was not ready. The better part of an expensive minute went by while Dody dithered about her unpreparedness and Janie and David, each with an ear pressed to the receiver, began to recognize the gibbering for what it was: a way out of telling them something.

"But you've been over there. You got into the apartment," Janie said, "and everything was all right, the phone and all? What do you mean *too tidy!*"

She did not laugh, however; there was something in Dody's tone, something more than her usual funny wail . . . bewilderment. Dody was not given to neurotic imaginings, she was too practical, down to earth. Yet for some reason—and she must have had some good reason—she had felt that she should call Aaron's school.

Janie clutched the receiver. "But he's got to be there. They've made a mistake."

Dody's misery came through all too clearly. David could picture her contorted, helpless expression. She had called their pediatrician, too. The doctor had not heard that Aaron was sick or anything.

"Of course, he doesn't have to go to school. There's no law. Not to nursery school," Janie argued desperately. "You have every right to keep a child at home. Or with you. Or take him to the zoo if you want to," she added wildly before her voice broke altogether.

One by one David pried her fingers from the telephone. "We're on our way," he told Dody. "We'll be home just as fast as we can get there."

"Please, if I can help you." Brock had effaced himself during the telephoning. Now with the lightest possible touch, as he would if she were asleep, not to startle her, he put his hand on Janie's arm. "There is something wrong."

"They can't just have disappeared. They've got to be somewhere, one place or the other. Benny's just taken him somewhere with her." Janie was as disoriented as if she had indeed been asleep. Then, aware of Brock, she said, "Benita. You remember Benita. She used to take care of me."

"But of course."

Janie seemed to find a shred of comfort in this common bond. "And now she's taking care of Aaron, our little boy."

"Ah, a son. I see. You have a son now. And Benita takes care of him. Is wonderful that. So he is safe, surely. You can have . . ." He paused, as if searching for a word. "What I mean to say: you can trust her?"

"Shouldn't we?" David had put down the telephone in time to hear the doubt in Brock's tone. "Shouldn't we trust her?" he asked sharply.

"After all these years . . ." Janie seemed incapable of finishing the sentence.

"Of course," Brock said in a placating tone, and then, "Only I wondered if she, too, thought you killed Luis. If perhaps she had not been able to forget."

Janie's eyes stretched with horror. "Do you think she loathes me . . . that much? Enough to hurt Aaron?"

"Now look here," David said furiously, furious with Brock. "Things were bad enough."

"Forgive me. I had no right. I do not know Benita to judge her. It is her brother I remember. They are not the same."

"Damn right," said David, sounding far more certain than he felt.

There was a miserable pause before Janie, agonizing aloud, said, "It always comes back to Manolo. From the very beginning: forcing you to run away, stealing from you, convincing me I'd killed Luis. Oh, God, what if Benita believes that? And why shouldn't she? Brother and sister, maybe they think exactly alike." She gave Brock a pleading look, begging him to argue, but he did not interrupt.

"And he keeps turning up. Everywhere," she told him. "Even at the Prado! There was a face in a painting that reminded me of him. I thought it looked like Benita, and then I was sure it looked like someone else, too, a man I'd seen hanging around our apartment house. That's why I called home in the first place. And there was nobody there. And I asked a friend to go over, and there still wasn't . . ."

"I think," David interjected quickly, "whichever of you speaks the best airline Spanish should be getting us on a flight out of here."

So it was Brock who next took over the telephone while David, as much for his own sanity as for Janie's, repeated in every way that he could think of that Aaron was fine, perfectly all right, couldn't be better. The fact that he was missing for a minute didn't mean a thing. It was just bad timing, one of those freaky things that can happen, a comedy of errors. Nothing sinister about it, there was some perfectly ordinary explanation. Then why, he wondered—although only to himself, pushing away his misgivings—was he going on so about it?

"You don't think she's kidnapped him?" Janie barely sounded the word. "Taken him away?"

David did his best to laugh this off. "Not likely," he said.

"If anyone hurt him . . ." Janie shook away the intolerable thought. "But she couldn't. She adores Aaron. And she wouldn't let Manolo touch him. She wouldn't, would she, David?"

He made a vague, comforting sound under cover of Brock's far more competent negotiations. It was, David thought, the final twist in this ill-fated trip that Brock had to extricate them from it.

To be able to help Janie was, however, Brock's great pleasure. This he made clear the next morning when as a final service he drove them to the airport. He had always hoped to repay Janie in some way.

"Always," he said, "I have remembered what you did for me. I was afraid I would never see you again. Always I have hoped to find you. When I came back here . . ."

"It was because of a girl. I heard that," she said.

"But of course," he teased with a warmth that flustered

her and made David all the more aware of the bond between them.

Brock's car, like his restaurant, had been recently acquired at second or third hand and indicated a certain faith in the future rather than any financial success he had yet achieved. Cramped in the back seat, David was critical. But the man himself was certainly attractive. His confidence sustained Janie. It was like a drug that had brought her through these last hours, that she was dependent on now, hooked. She clung to Brock emotionally and now that she had rediscovered him was unwilling to let go.

"You will come back here," he said at the airport.

"Will we?" Like a child she begged for unreasonable amounts of reassurance.

Brock took her hand and held it against his lips for a moment. "Everything will be all right," he said then. "You'll see. Your little boy is all right."

As last words often do, the words reechoed in David's ears and turned meaningless with repetition.

"But only to see the dancing girls," he said abruptly, "if we ever do."

Brock smiled politely, not understanding.

Flying west, the time difference meant that, by the clock, they made an extremely fast trip, a matter of a very few hours between departure and arrival. Even with the necessary change of planes they would be in New York in the afternoon, New York time. Yet David had never known distance and time to contort themselves so, not even in the cruelest nightmare. New York receded into infinity, as fast as they flew.

Only once before, and that was the night when Aaron was born, and their taxi was immobilized in crosstown traffic, had David felt such physical strain. His abdominal muscles contracting with every spasm of pain that clutched Janie, he felt that he had rocked the cab to the hospital himself, with his own body, inch by tortured inch.

He did not tell Janie what he was thinking. She lay back with her eyes closed, not restfully but squeezing the lids together as if willing everything to be all right and urging the plane on.

Lunch came because it was easier to accept than refuse. And because it was there, David worked at his chicken and picked the radish chips from the salad. When Janie opened her eyes, he put down his fork, although she did not seem to see the trays.

"Maybe we'll feel silly," she said. "Rushing home this way, giving up our trip. We'll get there and find out there's nothing wrong, and everyone will think we're out of our minds, won't they?"

He should have been able to say what she wanted him to say. "You'd better eat something," he said.

She noticed the food then for the first time, and when she had examined the choices, obediently broke open a roll. "Sometimes I don't believe it's happening, any of this. It's too incredible." She put the roll back on her tray. "Like a nightmare. But when do we wake up?"

The trays and the armrest made it impossible to put his arm around her. He reached over instead, buttered a piece of her roll and fed it to her.

She swallowed with difficulty. "Maybe I am overreacting. Exaggerating. I probably am. David, do you think I am?"

She looked to him for agreement, and when he hesitated she instantly defended herself. "But it's better to worry too much."

"Much better, I agree," he said.

She came unstuck immediately. "Nobody would hurt Aaron. Not even Manolo. Benny never would. Would she?"

This was the pattern all through the long flight, Janie dreaming up comforting ideas only to knock them down again, afraid not to worry enough. It was an exhausting, useless exercise. Lacking facts, she concocted a wide range of explanations for Benita's and Aaron's absence. As David had the night before, she made up benign excuses: simple misunderstanding or consistently bad timing, pure bad luck. Or there was Dody. At one point Janie blamed Dody for alarming them unduly.

"I don't mean that she'd frighten us on purpose—not consciously anyway—but, well, you know how she is."

He knew: scatterbrained maybe and silly on the surface, but practical, used to coping. She would not hit the panic button.

Janie's thoughts had leapt again. "Do you think we should have called Nat and Lynn?"

"I hadn't thought," he temporized. "Nat's a busy man. I don't like to bother doctors."

"That's not the real reason, is it?" She looked at him sharply.

He had enough to worry about; he did not want to talk about Nat Brandt just then. "No," he said.

"He makes you uncomfortable."

"You could say that. I feel a little like a fly on a pin."

"You don't like Lynn either."

Janie said this flatly and he answered more cautiously, not sure what she was getting at, "It's not that I dislike her exactly. There's not much to dislike, that's the thing. I don't feel that I really know her. Still, if she weren't your old school chum . . ."

"You don't like her being Aaron's godmother. Neither do I. Not now. Not any more. It scares me. When I think that if anything happened to us—to you and me—there'd be nobody else. My parents are too old to take care of Aaron full time, and there's no one in your family. Lynn's the only one. And she's wanted a child so badly . . . she'd have one . . ."

"Janie, don't! Please." He had not meant to shout at her, but he could not bear any more. He signaled to the stewardess that she should take away their trays.

From then on he found the flight almost unbearable. Unending. He had never before experienced such acute claustrophobia, such a trapped feeling. The brittle shell of the plane pressed in on him as he was hurtled along, dizzily, out of control. It was his turn to be unreasonable: he wanted to get off, and he was terribly afraid that he might disgrace himself by being sick.

Yet, looked back on, the flight seemed short and relatively easy. Guessing, speculating, suspecting could in some cases be better than knowing.

Chapter 13

They did not wait for the elevator to come down but dropped their bags in the lobby and sprinted up the stairs like long-distance runners, as if every second counted at the end.

The uncanny silence was the first thing they noticed. After the street racket and the hours of engine roar, the total quiet of the tightly closed apartment sounded wrong, as if their ears had not yet readjusted to sea level and needed to clear once more. The silence and—Janie remembered how this had bothered Dody—the tidiness. It was not a matter of scrubby-Dutch, hyper-conscientious housekeeping. This, although it was an elusive difference, was nasty neatness with a dulled and lifeless quality about it, a suggestion of undisturbed dust. And a revolting smell—of something left to rot in the stale and overheated air—but the garbage was the least of Janie's worries.

". . . at this time of day. They should be home, David." But they did not need to call out or look through the rooms to know that Aaron and Benita were not there.

The list of telephone numbers that Janie had left was beside the telephone in the kitchen, that and Dody's childishly printed note. Janie dialed Aaron's school from there with David standing by, watching her face for clues.

In a matter of days the room seemed to have undergone subtle changes so that he felt strange in it. He pushed open the casement window. What had been a thin rain at Kennedy now resounded in the air shaft and splashed like used wash water on the sooty ledge.

"You did? You're quite sure?" Janie said. "You saw him yourself?" Even then her face remained taut and resistant, as if she were afraid to believe, and she put down the phone inconclusively.

"He was in school today," she said in a doubtful tone. "She says he was picked up as usual. By a woman . . ."

"Then everything's fine. That's great. They'll be right along."

". . . nearly three hours ago," Janie said.

David followed her out of the kitchen, along the hall. Aaron's room was like the rest of the apartment: depersonalized, faultless yet wrong, his books and games and car collection arranged on the shelves, his bed precisely made. It took Janie a minute to see what was missing.

"That beat-up old stuffed turtle of his. And the owl. They're always on his bed. He can't sleep without the owl. Remember last summer, when we took him to the shore.

"It's a ratty old thing. Unsanitary. But Benny wouldn't throw it away, she couldn't," Janie went on in a jerky, distracted way, looking into the closet as she talked, then opening bureau drawers. "David . . . half his things are gone, his clothes!"

"To the laundry maybe? Couldn't they be out being

washed?" he said quickly, knowing better as he said it.

She shook her head. "No."

"Then I'm going to call the police."

"No, wait . . ."

He could not be sure why she stopped him, whether she really did not believe that this was a matter for the police. Or whether she knew that it was and could not face that knowledge yet. Would calling the police make Aaron's disappearance too real?

"We haven't even talked to Dody," Janie said.

But she did not go to the telephone. She stayed in Aaron's room as if there were something more to be learned there, some message in the air—or in the furniture; she kept patting things and running her hand over the red and blue bedspread, like a blind person.

"A kidnapper wouldn't do that, would he David? I mean an ordinary kidnapper."

"No, of course not."

"He wouldn't pack . . . and remember the stuffed animals . . ." Janie's voice broke. "Only Benny would do all that."

"Take it easy, baby." David caught at one of her hands and made her sit down with him on the edge of the bed. "Easy," he repeated. "We don't know anything yet. Aaron was in school today, remember?"

"She took him from there. That's why they're not back."

"But why today?"

"Because we were coming home. She must have heard. Dody must have reached her after all."

"I mean, why not months ago? If it's a matter of avenging her Luis's death."

"I don't know. But I think Manolo has been here. He's behind it somehow . . . oh, God."

As soon as she said Manolo's name, everything began to make a sickening kind of sense. What was it Janie had told Brock? It always came back to Manolo. It was as if she already knew, even then, that if there was anything wrong at home, Manolo was involved somehow.

David said very gently, "You think the two of them together?"

Janie nodded, her teeth locked.

"But what reason would *he* have? He's got nothing against you at this point. It's the other way around, if you ask me," David said angrily. "He got the jewels, didn't he? And your silence. You blotted out the whole thing."

"Manolo only does things for money," Janie said. "If he's got Aaron, that's why. He'll want money. Ransom."

"So help me, Janie, if I ever meet the bastard . . ." It was inexpressible, the murderous impulse David had at that moment, the black, unfocused hatred for a man he had never seen. First Janie and now Aaron, he thought savagely, and he imagined the satisfaction it would be to smash the man, literally, physically, to hurt him badly. His hands opened and closed inadequately as he suggested the one practical alternative, "We've got to call the police."

"We can't. That would be the worst thing . . . wouldn't it? I mean, for Aaron . . . if they've kidnapped him." She turned toward the window, her eyes blurring. Rain smeared the dirty glass and made everything worse. It was unbearable, the rain and the darkness closing in when Aaron was out there somewhere.

"I want Aaron. I want him back," Janie said, and it was

a pitiful, childish demand. "Did they remember his rubbers? And his yellow raincoat, do you think? David . . . ?"

He could not tell her what he was thinking. If Manolo, or Manolo and Benny, had Aaron, if they were holding him for money, wouldn't they say so? Make their filthy demands? Communicate somehow? But if they didn't know that Janie and David had come back early? Would they wait another week?

Not another week. David rejected that thought as impossible, beyond endurance. Couldn't they have left a note?

It was this thought—not a hope exactly, but at least an excuse for some form of action—that prompted him to look through the rest of the apartment. In their haste, he was reminded, they had gone no farther than the kitchen and Aaron's bedroom.

Janie started out with him, worrying still about Aaron's raincoat and rubbers, which struck him as good worry. "Easy enough to find out," he said. "If they're not in the coat closet, you'll know." This would keep her busy while he went on ahead. Because he suddenly did not want her with him. For no reason yet very strongly he felt that he must do this part alone.

The coat closet was in the entrance hallway, and it was always locked. Not that a lock ever stopped anybody— David could hear Janie's parents discussing the matter as they so frequently had—but it might serve as a deterrent. When they went away, they tried to remember to put their valuables in there, although Mrs. Vreeland, improvising in recent years, had been known to tuck the flat silver under the living room couch, or into the linen shelves under the sheets and towels as more subtle. Since the coat closet door had an irritating trick of locking itself automatically, the key was normally left in the lock or just overhead on the framing. David reached up for it and handed it to Janie.

He did not actually see her open the door. He had gone on into the living room when Janie made a strange sound, not a shriek, not at first, but a terrible inward yelp confused with the thud of a fast-closed door.

Then she screamed, repeatedly, like a deafening alarm that could not be turned off, and he found her pressed against the door as if it took all her strength to contain whatever was inside. Whatever horror; his first thought oddly was of something alive.

He had to be brutal to pry her away from the door—and to quiet her; the uncontrollable screams made him rougher than he had ever been. He shouted at her, to stop it for God's sake, and he finally slapped her harder than he meant to.

She was quieter then, whimpering, "No," over and over again. "No, David, don't. Don't open it," as he held her away from the door and turned the key.

The door swung toward him at once, pushed by the weight of the body that rolled out with it.

It was not Aaron. That, he realized, had been his inadmissible fear. It was definitely not Aaron. It was a grown man, black-haired. His shirt had been white; the blood on it had dried brown.

Backing away, David went rubbery with relief and could not suppress the involuntary sound that was almost like laughter. For a wild instant the fact that this was a total stranger made everything all right.

Janie looked brittle and white as plaster standing there

with both hands pressed over her mouth. David came to his senses then and pulled her away toward their bedroom, carefully steering her around the man who lay curled on his side and almost blocked the narrow hallway.

There was no discussion now and no hesitation. David called the police.

"We don't know him, do we?" he said when he had hung up, his call complete. He was incredulous still as he had been while he was telephoning, hearing himself report a strange body in his apartment, someone who had got himself in somehow during their absence and turned up dead in the hall closet. Unbelievable. He thought that he must have imagined the whole thing, that if he went back now and looked in the hall, he would see that there was nothing there. The police would be right along in any case.

"You don't know him?" he said more urgently.

Janie lay rigid and unblinking on the bed. "I want Aaron," she said exactly as she had before, as if nothing had happened in the meantime. "Now. I want him back now."

"Janie, listen. That man out there . . ."

Her eyes were fixed on the ceiling.

"Listen, it's important. I've got to know. He's not Manolo, is he?" David blurted out the question that he'd had to force himself to ask, afraid of the answer. He did not want the thing out there to have a name, to have any connection . . .

Janie rolled onto her side as if she were in pain. Like the man in the hall, but he felt nothing. "I thought Manolo had Aaron. Manolo and Benny," she said.

"The police will find Aaron. They'll have to know now."

She did not respond. She showed no sign of having heard him at all, nor of noticing his hand on her shoulder, help-lessly stroking. "It's going to be all right. There's nothing to worry about. You'll see. Aaron's fine. No one would hurt him. You know Benny wouldn't."

The soothing words were meaningless, automatic. All that David could think about was the dark shape in the hallway, filling it, filling the entire apartment, it seemed now. Whoever the man had been, he was very much in-volved in their life now. He had succeeded in making him-self very much David's problem.

"Janie . . . before the police get here, I think we ought to talk about this . . . get our story straight, you know? There'll be a hell of a lot of questions. We've got to make it damned clear that we're not mixed up in this thing. The police could misunderstand. We've got to be careful, be sure they don't get the wrong idea. It could be important. Janie . . . ?"

She lay perfectly still, apparently not hearing a word he said or feeling the pressure of his hand. He shook her and repeated her name loudly.

"Where could they have gone?" she said then.

It was as if she had sealed herself off. Retreating from this final shock, defending herself as she had once before, she seemed to have obliterated the dead man, to have erased him altogether.

David knew then what he had to do, whether he wanted to or not. His fingers dug into Janie's shoulder unfelt. He released her and pulled the telephone directory from the drawer of the bedside table.

He tried Nat Brandt's office first and when the answering

service came on, he hung up rudely and dialed the home number.

Nat's voice was always low, professionally modulated, neutral. He could not allow himself to sound surprised, so that when he said, "Well, David," genially, it was as if he had been expecting this call.

"But you are back early?" he said.

"Look, I'm sorry. I mean, I'm sorry to bother you like this, but could you come over . . . right away? It's Janie."

Clumsily as David said this, Nat humored him. "But of course," he said. "Aaron . . ."

"He's only part of it," David put in and then, stumbling over his own words, "How did you know?"

"He's anxious to see you, too. Naturally. He has been counting the days."

David could imagine the indulgent smile. The superior, smug, knowing smile. "So he's with you," he said stiffly. "That's where he's been all this time, while Janie was going out of her mind, worrying. You've had him right along!" His anger exploded as he saw Janie's distorted face turned toward him, questioning, afraid to believe what she had guessed.

He nodded and said into the phone, "He *is* all right, isn't he? I can assure Janie of that. Good of you to let us know," he added acidly.

"But we assumed that you did know. From what Benita said."

"Then why the hell have you been hiding him? Why wasn't he in school yesterday?"

"Surely that is not so important, to miss a day now and then. I believe that he had a slight cold. Lynn worried." Nat was reasonable, detached, as if David were one of his patients. He never allowed himself to be offended. "But you said that Aaron was part of it. There's more? You wanted me for another reason?"

Janie's eyes were closed again but with a prayerful look, as if she were giving thanks, and her whole face was smooth with relief. "I must tell Dody right away," she murmured. There was still no indication that she remembered the man who lay curled in the hall.

"Yeah," David told Nat. "Another reason. You'd still better come over. On the double."

For the first time Nat was unsure. "And bring Aaron? Or not?"

"Oh, God, no. Don't bring Aaron. You'll see . . . when you get here. And hurry," David urged. "The police have just arrived."

Chapter 14

The door could not be opened all the way without nudging the body. Unavoidably, it came up against the mound of the buttocks, so that the first two policemen edged past, their faces grim, and the doorman hesitated to come in at all until he realized that he was about to be shut out entirely.

David found the scene unreal. Somehow, now that they had found Aaron safe and sound, inexplicably fine, the whole nightmare should have ended. Like their black worry about Aaron, the hideous object should have vanished. But it was very much there, filling the entry, all too obvious to the men who stood pressed against the wall, looking down at it with distaste.

There was an element of disbelief in their attitude, too.

"Like he just fell out of the closet," one of them said, "right? That's what you're saying. Like you never seen him before and he gets in here. He gets into your closet and dies on you." He looked intently at David for a moment, then gave the doorman an equal scrutiny. "That figure?"

"It has a way of locking itself automatically. Accidentally. The closet door," David suggested. "If he meant to hide in there, for some reason . . ."

"It's possible." The probability, however, went unsaid as hardly worth mentioning.

"We were away, my wife and I, on a trip. We were in Spain."

"So no one was home, you mean? The apartment was empty?"

David hesitated for a fraction of a second, then said, "Yes, as it turned out. My little boy . . ."

"I can vouch for that," the doorman interrupted, snatching at the chance to be helpful. Ingratiating, David thought, as if there might be a worthwhile tip in it, only this time it was a matter of making character with the police. His name was Walter, although David, who had never warmed to the man, avoided calling him anything.

"There was this lady come over," he elaborated now, "said she'd been calling and calling, no answer, and could she go in and see about the phone. I could've told her there wasn't anybody home, hadn't been anybody in to pick up the mail or anything, but she had to see for herself, and seeing's how she was a friend of yours and you was going to be talking to her again, long distance," he accused David, "I let her go in.

"Not out of my sight though," he added hastily. "Not with two kids."

One of the officers stopped this pious disclaimer. "And everything looked okay to you then? You didn't notice anything wrong."

"I'd a reported it if I did."

"Sure you woulda." The policeman had a quick, mean grin.

"But I didn't go in myself. I just unlocked the door for her."

David listened with mild interest, amused by the doorman's wriggling. He could imagine Dody rattling in, Walter condescending. But he could not feel that any of this was relevant, least of all that it had anything to do with him. The dead man lying curled on the floor so altered the atmosphere, he could believe, briefly, that he had blundered into the wrong apartment.

"You will be getting him out of here," he said, "the body?"

In due course, he was told; there were procedures to be followed first—photographs, fingerprints, a strict order of events. You didn't just toss dead bodies around, not even the foreign-looking ones. You didn't touch 'em if you could avoid it. You left that to the coroner's boys, let them worry about who the guy was, cause of death and like that, and the stretcher when they were good and ready.

Again David felt remote, not quite convinced, a little as if he were watching all this on television, but inattentively, half his mind elsewhere. The police routines seemed vaguely familiar, like any spectator sport. But he had no need to participate, until he became aware—with a nasty start, not sure what he had missed—that the shorter of the policemen was expecting something, his mouth sarcastic.

"I thought it might save us some time, is all, if we talked to her now. If you went and got her, like *now,*" he repeated. "Or you want me to?"

"No, no. It's just that . . . I mean, my wife is resting.

This has been a terrible shock to her, you can imagine, finding this . . ."

"She's already seen it then. So it shouldn't be too hard, just to verify."

David was afraid to refuse. Like the doorman's, his instincts told him not to antagonize the police, no matter what, to give a semblance of candor, of complete cooperation. Yet Janie, in the state she was in . . .

He walked slowly back to their bedroom, and quietly. There was the chance, the hope, that Janie really was resting, that released at last from fears for Aaron, she might even be asleep.

She was not. She had been on the phone to Dody—he did not ask her how much she had said—and now she was standing at the window of the darkening room, holding back the curtain, outlined there against the diffused gleam of city lights. This room, like the living room, overlooked the street, which was shiny wet now, shimmering with double images, the traffic hissing.

Watching beside her for a moment with his arm around her, David felt her steely tension. "He's still out there, isn't he?" she asked. "In the hall. They haven't taken him away yet."

"They want you to have a look at him. I know you've already seen him," he said before she could protest. "It's just a formality, part of their routine. They just want to make sure that you don't know him, that you've never seen him before. That's all you have to tell them."

"I didn't look at his face before. I couldn't."

"No, of course not." His arm tightened in sympathy and he turned her away from the window. "It will only take a minute. A quick look for the record, just to confirm that we can't help with the identification. He's nothing to do with us. Then they can get on with it, get him out of here. . . .

"You understand?" he said anxiously; there was something about the quality of her silence.

Janie nodded. "A quick look."

"There's no problem. Walter has already sworn that the apartment was empty. And Dody can back him up on that, if necessary, though I doubt that it will be. Everything points to an ordinary break-in, only this one backfired. My guess is there were at least two of them and they got in a fight . . . or maybe he was dead when he got here, they just needed a place to put him. I don't know.

"The main thing is, he's no friend of ours. He just happened in here because no one was home. And the sooner you do your bit, the sooner the police can get on with theirs and start cleaning up the mess. And Aaron can come home," David coaxed.

The body, as it rolled out of the closet, had fallen onto its right side with the head toward the dining room and so turned on the twisted neck that the dead man appeared to be looking up, but ducking slightly, grotesquely coy. The two policemen and Walter made way in silence—introductions hardly seemed in order—so that Janie would have a clear view.

She bent over, her own head tilted sidewise as if, making every effort to recognize him, she needed to see him face to face. She held her hands clutched together in front of her with such pressure that David could see their color blotching, wine red and white. She stayed that way longer than he would have thought bearable, conscientiously studying the grisly face, and when she straightened, whether it was the sight or the smell that had sickened her, her own face was ghastly.

"Are you all right?" It was an idiot question, she so patently was not, and David moved to steady her.

"Look familiar?" The cop had skeptical, prepared-for-the-worst eyes, and he watched Janie closely while he waited for an answer. "He does, doesn't he?" he prompted at last, confidently. "You've seen him before someplace. You know who he is, right?"

"Can't you see she's in shock?" David tried to forestall him.

"I didn't ask you, did I? I was talking to her. Okay, lady."

"I'm not sure," Janie began slowly. "You see, he does look familiar."

"Janie . . ." David warned. "Stick to what you *know*. They only want facts."

"But it looks like him. That same kind of face."

"Janie, for God's sake, don't fool around. You're just guessing. You haven't seen him since you were a child."

"Okay, you. Okay." It was one of the policemen.

"My husband," Janie told him softly, "thinks I'm hallucinating. He thinks I've got an obsession or something because I keep seeing someone, a face."

"Like this one?" The officer pointed with his shoe.

She nodded. "First here. I saw him across the street. I thought he was watching our apartment."

"And then?"

"At the Prado. It's an art museum, in Madrid. In a painting. It looked exactly like him. And then I realized that it also looked like Benita, our Spanish maid, enough like her to be her brother, and I thought maybe it was her brother, a man named Manolo Santos."

The policeman was clearly dubious now. "So you think maybe this is him, your maid's brother, this Manolo? That's what you're saying?"

Janie nodded again, miserably. "It's true, I hadn't seen him for years. But I thought he might have come to New York."

The policeman turned to David. "So what's wrong with that? What do you care, she keeps seeing this guy? It's not like he's some old boyfriend or something she's got on the brain. Or is it?" he asked abruptly.

"Not at all like that," said Janie. "I loathed him."

The policemen looked pleased. David groaned. "You don't understand," he tried to tell them. "My wife had nothing to do with this."

"No? Well, then you haven't got anything to worry about, have you? So you won't mind spelling a few names for us."

It was while these notes were being taken that the front door buzzer sounded, harsh and startlingly close. David was glad of the interruption.

"Well, that gives us something to start on," he was told. "One good thing about foreigners, Immigration can tell us if your friend came into the country lately." He eyed Janie once more, then opened the door.

Nat Brandt's voice was always beautifully controlled. Even now he did not raise it but said, "Good Lord," distinctly as he was eased into the hallway. "It's all right, I'm Dr. Brandt," he assured the police. Then hastily, to clarify his position, he added that he was not, very definitely not, the medical examiner.

"I'm a psychiatrist, actually. And a friend," he explained. "I hurried over the minute Mr. Ingstrom called me."

"Oh." The policeman scratched himself. "Yeah. Sure. It figures."

Chapter 15

With the bedroom door closed, they were less aware of the increasing police activity in the hallway. Or at least they heard it less distinctly than they had. David was conscious of further arrivals, different voices, and the inhuman sounds of equipment. He tried not to visualize the procedure, the photographing and diagraming—were they dusting for fingerprints?—the ultimate removal of the dreadful object. Instead he narrowed his attention as much as possible to Janie, who no longer sounded the least bit confused or fey, but cold and clear.

And caustic. "That was great, what you just did for my credibility," she said. "Thanks a lot."

Nat raised his hands, defending himself. "My dear lady, if I have offended you . . . But what would you have me say? That I *am* the medical examiner?"

This mild and somehow condescending joke did not go over.

"So now they *know* I'm a crazy lady. They weren't quite sure before, they only suspected."

"Forgive me, if I have embarrassed you. Perhaps I spoke hastily in the circumstances, having stumbled over a body." Nat smiled minimally. "David should have warned me."

The civilized façade was almost more than David could take. For an instant—a barbaric and immature instant, no one needed to tell him—he wondered if a well-aimed fist would dislodge that smile, if Nat would continue to be so urbane, so understanding. Probably.

"Anyway," David conceded, "you came at a good time. Janie was having a fit of honesty, telling the police more than she knew. About our friend out there, the one you stumbled over."

"Friend?" Nat's eyebrows went up receptively.

"She had an idea it was Benny's brother. A character called Manolo. I say it could be anybody. A common Latin type. I hope to hell it is," he added with feeling.

"Yes, I can see that. To keep this unpleasantness at a distance." Nat glanced toward Janie. "Yes, a total stranger would be better."

"At least," David said, "I don't see claiming him on spec. Or blurting out how you hated him. That does seem like asking for it, volunteering . . ."

He was abruptly stopped by Janie's expression. It was as if she was the one he had slugged, by unaccountably turning on her, aligning himself with Nat. She stood with her back to the window, hands gripping the sill behind her, looking cornered and outnumbered.

"Janie, listen . . . I'm sorry."

"But surely," Nat intervened, "there are other ways of finding out who he is. He would carry some identification."

"That's what they should be getting to. Right about

123

now," David said. "Apparently you don't just go poking through the pockets in a case like this. You wait for the medical examiner. We should be hearing pretty soon. Meanwhile . . ."

He pushed up his glasses, temporizing. He was not sure what he meant to say. There was a lot about Spain. There had been no chance to tell Nat about their trip and all that they had learned in Bilbao. About Janie's extraordinary meeting with Brock . . . the facts about Luis's death and how they had at last freed Janie from her strange buried guilt . . . about Manolo.

Before he could say anything more, however, Janie had rounded on Nat. "Meanwhile," she said, "what I want to know is how you got into this."

"But David called me."

"No. I mean how did you happen to have Aaron? Practically the minute our backs were turned."

"Dear lady." Again Nat raised his hands, fending her off. "It was your idea surely. Entirely your idea."

"Mine!"

"Yours." He smiled regretfully at this absurd exchange. "We were given to understand, by *your* maid, that she had brought Aaron to us at your suggestion, when she was called away."

"Called away where?"

For the first time Nat looked uneasy. His smooth surface altered as he studied Janie, scowling. "You really do not know about this. You are not"—he paused for an uncomfortable interval—"well, forgetting something?"

David was startled by his own quick anger. "Let's not have any more psychiatric crap. We've been through that, all through that and Janie's fine. She's not forgetting a thing. Now what's this about Benny being called away?"

"She said . . . no, I correct myself. Lynn understood your maid to say that she had heard from you, that her father was critically ill and she must come at once, that you had told her to leave the boy with us."

"Lynn told you that? How very creative."

There was no mistaking Janie's hostility. Nat was white, drawn tight. His personal honor, generations of his family honor, might have been in question. "We do not tell lies," he said.

"But we never called Benny. We tried, but . . . Anyway, none of it's true. Her father's fine, we saw him. We certainly didn't tell her to come over. Or to leave Aaron with you."

"Damn right," David said loudly, and found himself moving to stand next to Janie in a token closing of ranks that gave final form to the standoff.

Fractionally, Nat relaxed his shoulders. But not his voice. "There is the possibility, I suppose, that there has been a slight misunderstanding."

"Slight!" Janie exploded, conceding him nothing.

"Because of language. My wife is not a linguist. Your maid speaks limited English. She may have explained badly."

"But explained what?" Janie put in rapidly. Her own tone was relenting, however, puzzled. Whatever thought had occurred to her, she seemed to reject it, then somewhat unwillingly, come back to it. "Lynn *is* Aaron's godmother," she admitted. "Benita could have overheard, half understood . . . about Lynn's taking care of Aaron, I mean, if anything ever happened to us."

"And what exactly was supposed to have happened to us?" David wanted to know. "Jumping the gun a little, wasn't she?"

"No, that's not what I meant. Now you're the one who's jumping to conclusions. All I meant was, if she needed help, someone to take care of Aaron, she would think of Lynn. But . . . I know," she said, looking wanly at David and forestalling his next question, "but *why?* Why did she need help?"

"I can think of one obvious possibility." He tilted his head in the direction of the front hall. "I'd have moved out myself."

"No, you wouldn't. You'd do exactly what you did do, call the police. Then where *is* she?" It was an accusation, directed at Nat, as if he were basically to blame.

David intervened. "Not if I'd put him there myself, I wouldn't. I don't think I'd call the police if I'd had a hand in his death. If I'd murdered the bloke, say," he added as Janie gaped at him. The facetious note was wasted on her. "Or then again, maybe I would, to prove my innocence, or something," he trailed off.

"You think Benny . . . Oh, David."

David turned to Nat. "When did she leave here? When did she bring Aaron to you?"

"Frankly . . ." Nat's hands moved emptily, at a loss without an appointment pad. "Lynn would remember more accurately, but let me think. You left about a week ago?"

"Almost exactly."

"Then I think for about four days we have had Aaron. What I remember is that it seemed very soon after your going. Lynn and I talked about that. We thought that you

126

must have had the bad news of the old father's illness very soon after you arrived in Spain. It was too bad."

"About four days," David said. "And how long has that guy been dead?"

"That may be difficult to establish precisely. In the circumstances," Nat said.

"But it could have happened after she left."

"Oh, yes. Or before."

"Then where did she go?" Janie demanded. "When you thought she was rushing off to Spain? She left Aaron with Lynn, and then what? She can't have been here. Dody or the doorman, someone would have seen her. But where on earth is she now?"

"Good question," said David.

"If you'll allow me"—Nat had been watching Janie with anxiety—"I would suggest that you leave all these good questions to the police. Not to upset yourself. When the victim is identified, when the Spanish woman is found, then everything will be answered, is that not so?"

His enunciation and his equally precise smile, plainly designed to lull, seemed to have the opposite effect on Janie. She looked furious, and when he prescribed "A tranquilizer perhaps," her refusal was emphatic.

"Then about Aaron?" Continuing sounds in the hallway seemed to answer Nat's question.

"Yes, if you'd keep him one more night," David said, and with an uneasy sense that there was a great deal more to be said, he added, "Thanks, Nat," unconvincingly.

The formality of showing Nat to the door was made doubly awkward by the police presence. It was a matter of picking a way through without touching anything. Nat, in the lead, repeatedly excused himself.

"Just a minute, sir." He was stopped at the door.

With a gesture that David could not help admiring, Nat produced a card. "You can always reach me," he assured the officer, "if you need me."

Chapter 16

Janie was still at the window, looking down into the street as if the shifting patterns of light, even the limited variety of the traffic signals, provided some essential diversion. She turned when David came back. "He's gone?"

"Nat has, yes. But not far. He made it clear he can always be reached."

"I wish Aaron were here. I don't like his being with them. I want to see him, make sure he's all right. He is all right, isn't he? David? You're sure?"

As a substitute for answering, he put an arm around her and guided her toward the bed. She sat down obediently, but on the very edge, tensed. "I can't help wondering about Lynn, her part in all this."

"Including junior out there?" David nodded toward the hall. It was difficult to put a name to the thing.

"I was thinking more about Aaron. And how badly Lynn has wanted a child."

"She'd have been welcome to baby-sit, anytime."

"A child of her own. She tried desperately to have one,

you know. I think she's about given up. I don't say that this is a rational solution exactly," Janie forestalled David's protest, "but people do get obsessed. When they want something badly enough. I've read about women snatching babies right out of their carriages."

"She could have adopted a baby."

"Easier said than done. It can take years. And they're terribly fussy; lots of couples don't qualify. Maybe because Nat's so much older . . ."

"And a psychiatrist at that." Even a hypothetical failure on Nat's part cheered David briefly. "Even then, sweetie, I can't honestly see Lynn being driven to kidnapping."

"Can't you? Think about it a minute. Remember the night they were here for dinner, the night before we left? Aaron was passing things, remember? Being his most beguiling, and Lynn could hardly take her eyes off him."

"As a matter of fact, I do remember. I remember thinking how matronly she seemed, yet somehow not motherly . . . not at all easy with children the way Dody is, for instance."

Janie nodded. "Then what if she started fantasizing about Aaron, imagining that he was hers? She knew that we were going away."

"But only for a couple of weeks."

"Long enough, if she moved quickly. Don't you see? We're hardly out of the country before Benny gets a call. She's to hurry off to Spain, leave Aaron with Lynn."

"You think she lied to Nat about that? Do you think Lynn made it all up?"

"I think Lynn may well have made the call herself. Anything to get Benny out of the way. Then there was nothing to stop her."

"Until we got back, and then the whole stupid lie would come out." David paused and added uncomfortably, "Or would it? I suppose she could always say there'd been a misunderstanding. That's what Nat seems to think. In the end it would just be her word against Benny's."

"Her word, period," Janie said bitterly, "as long as Benny isn't here to defend herself."

"Right. But what's the point? She has Aaron for a couple of weeks at the most, and then we come back and reclaim him."

"That's assuming that we do come back."

"Why wouldn't we come back? I don't see Lynn stopping us." He spoke quickly in a matter-of-fact tone for Janie's benefit.

But his own imagination was going berserk all at once. Lynn—the pale, blank, pigeonlike Lynn!—had, through some nightmare distortion, become a monster, capable of the most sinister manipulation. She, or she and Nat in cahoots, had engineered everything: the whole trip. Theirs and then Benita's to get everyone out of the way. Somehow then Lynn was tied up with Brock—through Nat, of course! Two Germans. So . . . ? So Brock was to do them in, eliminate both Aaron's parents. But he hadn't. He had been kindness itself, pulling Janie out of the bay, driving them to the airport. He had not planted a bomb on their plane. There had been nothing of the sort.

With the surge of relief that waking up can bring, David recognized his fantasies for what they were—crazy, twisted nonsense. Ashamed of himself, he tried to sound all the more reasonable.

"Anyway, we are back, safe and sound. No one tried to stop us."

"No, but look what we came back to. That awful man, David, in the hall. What if they blame him on us, if they say we killed him, if they convict us . . ."

The melodramatic words came out wtih difficulty. Tight-throated, Janie finished on a little snort that was like an ugly laugh. "We wouldn't just be unfit parents, we'd be very unavailable."

"Janie, stop it!" Aware suddenly of the proximity of the police, David lowered his voice. "We weren't anywhere near here, not within thousands of miles. We couldn't have had anything to do with that guy if we wanted to. And we certainly couldn't have stuffed him into the closet after we got back, if that's what you're thinking. It's easy enough to prove that we've only been back a few hours—and he's been in there a hell of a lot longer than that. It's obvious, from the state of the body."

"I know. He must have been there for days. That's what I mean. We couldn't possibly have locked him in the closet today." Janie was very still, with a fatalistic sort of calm, and sounded altogether rational. "But what about before we left, David?"

Totally and terribly rational. David felt a strange prickle of fear run down his back.

"Will they be able to tell whether he died after we left— or just before?" Janie asked quietly.

"I don't know." There had to be a better answer, some incisive rebuttal to all this. It was bad enough to find a stray body in the coat closet, but he'd be damned if he'd take the rap. It was ludicrous, it couldn't be happening. He would think why in a minute. "Good God," he said.

The tap on the door was soft enough, hardly more than a blunt finger against the wood, but the simultaneous voice came through as harsh and eminently hostile.

"We'd like to talk to you now."

There were two of them, and these were new men. David thought for a moment that they were reporters—they had that look—until they flipped their credentials at him. They were police detectives Grazzi and Fitts. He learned their names later; at the time his mind was not on their brusque introductions.

"In here?" he said.

"Nope. If you don't mind . . . they've finished up out here, all clear, and there's something I'd like to show you. Nothing like that," he added as Janie shrank back onto the bed.

"But have you found out who he is? Was," said David, "and what in hell he was doing here?"

"We're working on it." The larger and more communicative of the two, the man who turned out to be Grazzi, was also the more rumpled. His unbuttoned coat revealed a shirt ballooning out of his belt like a second stomach. Fitts, the lighter-haired, lighter-weight one, was the passive observer squinting at David, then at Janie.

"Not so hard to guess what he was doing here." Grazzi's hand, pudgy and closed, moved suggestively, almost as if he were shaking dice. "The interesting thing is that otherwise his pockets are empty. Picked clean, no billfold, no nothing to identify him. You wouldn't know anything about that? You wouldn't have touched him?"

Grazzi's manner was easy, unhurried. It was Fitts who

glared edgily.

"Not with a pole," David said.

"It makes it harder, of course, not knowing who a victim was. But it makes one thing pretty clear, doesn't it?" Grazzi waited.

"Not to me it doesn't," David admitted.

Obliged Grazzi went on then. "I'd say it's just about certain that our man didn't walk himself into that closet. Not without help he didn't. I mean he wasn't hiding in there or anything like that and got himself locked in by accident. He was put there, and he wasn't in any shape to object at the time. Out cold probably, and bleeding. You know how head wounds are, they bleed a lot. There's a lot of blood in the closet."

"We didn't notice," David said faintly.

"There were two of them. At least two." Janie was animated, flushed. "That's what David said before. He must have had a friend, an accomplice, and they had a fight. So it was the friend who didn't want the body identified. Naturally. This way there's no connection, nothing to lead you to . . . to him. The attacker. The murderer?"

Grazzi was watching her closely, with some of Fitts's dubious intensity. If he had heard about her earlier near-identification of the body, he did not mention it now but said only, "Yeah. And then there's this thing I wanted you to see. If you'd come out here . . ."

Following him down the hall from their bedroom and past the front entry toward the dining room, they were acutely aware of the area of floor where the body had lain. With Janie's arm drawn through his, David felt her flinch and shy around the spot. Not that there was any visible

134

stain. There was no blood here, but David thought that he would never forget the look of the corpse as it had been, grossly curled there.

"In here," the large detective directed.

At first glance there was nothing of interest in the dining room, only the same sterile tidiness that affected the rest of the apartment. The small walnut table was bare, with two Italian chairs neatly tucked under it, and the other chairs primly flanking the narrow sideboard. The sideboard itself held a cluster of candleholders, a squat and heavy silver-plated pair, worn almost down to the copper, and an assortment of brightly glazed ceramic ones. In front of the candlesticks was a large square tile, blue and a dull brownish gold, the seal of the city of Bilbao.

"You see that?"

"Yes, of course," Janie told him. "It's always been there. For hot things. My parents brought it from Spain years ago."

"How long's it been broken?"

"I didn't know it was." Janie had to lean over it closely—not touching it, the policemen made clear, stopping her hand as she reached for it—to see the almost imperceptible crack that was like a fine brownish hair lying across the face of the tile. "I don't think it *was* broken when we left," she said.

"Maybe not." Grazzi gave the words an incomprehensible gravity. "Maybe not," he repeated, his eyes moving from Janie to David and then to his partner. "Show them," he said. "Carefully. We just might be looking at a murder weapon. It's already been dusted. No prints, natch."

Fitts handled the tile with the utmost respect by the extreme corners. The jagged break was complete. The brown felt backing adhered to one half tenuously, so that most of the rough underside of the tile was exposed. It was surprisingly pocked, deeply gouged.

"I don't get it," David said.

"You will," Grazzi promised somewhat grimly and with the same heavy humor added, "Apparently somebody did."

It was then that he opened his fist to display the emerald. Even encrusted as it was in bits of some rough, grayish plasterlike substance and nested in Grazzi's fleshy palm, it was a startling object, large and brilliant.

"Looks to me," the detective said, "like it was stuck inside. Same cement or whatever it was, you can see that. And it wasn't the only one, from the look. You see all the hollowed out places. Could've been quite a little fortune stashed away in there, all neat and tidy under the felt. But this is all we found. It was in his pocket."

Grazzi then produced a mean little smile for Janie's benefit, jiggling the emerald close to her face. "For hot things, you said. Isn't that what you said the tile was for?"

The silent Fitts snorted appreciatively.

"I just wondered," Grazzi went on, "if you was thinking of hot rocks, for instance. If maybe you smuggled in a few extra souvenirs. You, or your folks maybe."

Janie stepped back, away from his offensive hand, shaking her head. "I had no idea," she said. "I don't understand," and seemed incapable of continuing.

David took over then with all the indignation he could muster in a hurry. "And we're supposed to have kept them lying around . . . for a rainy day or something. Is that what you're saying? Don't be stupid. Anyway, my wife was

136

a child when they came back to this country. Her father was a respected Foreign Service officer. He's retired now, living in California, he and my wife's mother. Call them up if you don't believe me." David wound down abruptly under the combined observation of the two detectives.

"Go on," Grazzi encouraged him.

But it was Janie who responded in a puzzled tone, "I did have an emerald when I was little."

Grazzi's eyebrows rose in silence.

"I lost it. At least I thought they were all lost, an emerald and some diamonds that were given to me."

"By your fairy godmother?"

"By a German boy I knew. A refugee, a deserter, whatever you want to call him. A lot of them came into Spain at the end of the war, when they knew they'd lost."

"One of those war criminals?"

"He was a boy. I don't know about his commanding officer, maybe he was. He was the one who stole the plane. And the jewels. He was killed when they crash-landed. My friend ended up with the jewels."

Grazzi waited.

"And he gave me some. I'd helped him. I'd taken him food."

"I see," Grazzi said without conviction. "And then you just sort of lost them. An emerald and a few diamonds. Wow."

Janie managed to smile. "I was six years old. I had no sense of values."

"People don't always remember. I mean, things that happen when they're that young, people's memories are spotty. You don't think you could've hidden the jewels in the tile yourself, and then forgotten?"

Janie shook her head. "I don't think I was clever enough. Anyway, why would I? I'm sure I didn't know that they were especially valuable. We played with them! I thought they were pretty, but . . ."

Straining to remember, she chewed on her lower lip for a moment, then shook her head again. "No. If I'd hidden them in the tile, I'm sure I'd remember. Seeing the tile around all these years. It's always been around. It would have reminded me, wouldn't it? Wouldn't it?" she appealed at the last to David.

"Sure it would. Anyway, that's all ancient history now. What difference does it make?"

"Plenty," said Grazzi, looking dangerously pleased by the question, "as you'll see in a minute. What I'm getting at is who knew what was in that tile. Because it didn't just get broken accidentally, you know. Not in my book it didn't. That's a good thick tile. Someone gave it quite a whack to break it in two that way. And it's tough. It held up when someone went after someone with it. Tough, and sharp enough apparently to do a lot of damage. You see the brownish stuff along this edge here? Hardly shows unless you're looking for it. Blood, we're pretty sure."

Having bent close over the tile, Janie straightened, swallowing rapidly. "Oh," she said.

"Interesting, isn't it? Like we've got the motive and the weapon all in one, right here in our hands. It makes it interesting, unusual like. It also makes me think our nameless victim didn't just happen in here. It makes me think he knew exactly what he was looking for. And so did somebody else, wouldn't you say?

"So now, Mrs. Ingstrom, let's have a little more 'ancient history,' shall we? Think hard. Who, aside from you and your parents, would have known about this tile? Anyone else? You have any brothers or sisters?"

Janie shook her head with such evident misery, it was obvious that she was holding back a painful answer—or considering a lie; for a bad moment David was afraid that by refusing to tell the truth she would implicate herself hopelessly.

"All right, who?" Grazzi persisted.

"We had maids," she said at last.

"One of whom stayed on with my wife's family when they came back to the States," David supplied.

"And she is now . . . ?"

"Back in Spain, we think. It's a little hard to explain."

"Try me," said Grazzi, pulling out chairs and arranging them around the table. When everyone was seated, he said, "Okay. Now . . ." and he listened patiently while Janie, somewhat erratically, summarized what she knew about Benita's probable actions.

"Then she was here when you left?" the detective recapitulated. "She and the boy. But you have reason to believe that she left soon afterwards. You couldn't reach her and a Mrs. uh . . ." he consulted his notes, "a Mrs. Emmet couldn't find her, and the doorman hadn't seen her. You only know that she left your son with Dr. and Mrs. Brandt. And Mrs. Brandt was given to understand that the subject, this Benita, had been summoned to Spain. By you, but you say you didn't make any call like that, right?"

"And I can't think who would have—certainly not her father or anyone in Bilbao, we were right there, we would have known. It doesn't make sense, unless . . ."

"It doesn't make sense, period," David interjected firmly.

Grazzi raised a large, cautioning hand. "Unless what, Mrs. Ingstrom?"

Flushed now and rebellious, Janie said, "Sorry, David, but I can't help what I think," and turned back to Detective Grazzi. "I think Mrs. Brandt might have made the call herself."

"Why?"

"Because she was the only one who gained by it. Don't you see?" Stubbornly, but disconcerted by the expressions of the two policemen, Janie persisted, "She got Aaron that way, our little boy. By sending Benita off . . ."

There was a subtle variation in Grazzi's manner, a softening. "Dr. Brandt is a psychiatrist, I believe. And you have consulted him, as a patient?"

"No, no. Only as a friend. Tell them, David."

Again the detective's hand deterred David. "But the kid's all right, isn't he? They took good care of him. Didn't I hear he's staying there another night?"

"Yes. I know. I wish he weren't. I wish he were here." She seemed to give up, suddenly exhausted, and rested her head on her folded arms. Almost immediately, however, her head bobbed up. "Do you think he knows anything? Aaron, I mean. Could he have seen anything, or heard anything?"

"How old?"

"He's almost six, nearly the same age that I . . ."

Fitts, apparently expecting a signal from his partner, pushed back his chair. On the table in front of him, the tile had been reassembled, the felt smoothed into place and the halves fitted together so that from a slight distance the break was invisible. It was almost as if the damage had been undone, or as if nothing had happened.

"You want I should go get him?" Fitts asked.

"Oh, yes. Yes, please," Janie said. "I'll go with you."

Grazzi's expressive hand motioned her back into her chair. "I'd rather you didn't, ma'am. I'd rather you stayed right where you are so we can talk some more."

He was elaborately polite, considerate in a kid-gloved way that David found far more worrisome than rudeness could ever have been. And David, with a feeling that he could read Grazzi's mind, was certain all at once that he understood the man. He adores Janie, David thought. He's wild about her and handling her tenderly because he thinks she's crazy. Crazy enough to kill a man and shut him away in her own coat closet?

Dimly, on the basis of fictional murder—and television—it occurred to David that Janie should probably have a lawyer. As quickly as he thought this, he began to discount the idea as extreme, even hysterical. They had not called on a lawyer since early in their marriage, when they had made out routine new wills. David could not recall the man's name, and in any case he could not imagine him—the pale, orderly, distinctly academic type—as any match for Grazzi and a highly unsavory corpse.

"Just a couple more questions." Grazzi was gently reassuring.

Fitts had left, supplied with the Brandts' address, and Janie seemed happier. Out from under his constant scrutiny they resettled themselves at the table in a slightly relaxed mood.

"About your maid first. We'll want to talk to her, of

course, so any help you can give us in finding her . . ."

Janie's answers were direct, factual. She rattled off Don Pedro's address and her own parents' California address and telephone number without hesitation. Only when she came to describing Benita did she have difficulty.

"Well, you know, middle-aged and sort of heavy and dark and . . . Spanish-looking! If I could find a snapshot . . ."

"It would help," Grazzi agreed. "So far the description fits just about anybody. Including the victim," he murmured, smiling oddly.

"I know." To David's immense relief, she did not go on about the resemblance but pushed away from the table and stood up, saying, "I'll just see if I can find a picture."

Grazzi followed her closely down the length of the hall to the child-sized room that had been Benita's. David did not go with them. He stayed at the table, staring at the thin brown line across the Bilbao tile as if it could show him the way out of this.

Chapter 17

The photographs could never have been very good. Now, browned and curled, they had a dim and depressingly antique look. There were two of them, apparently taken at the same time by a sidewalk photographer. Janie had found them in a stationery box in a bottom drawer in Benita's room, part of a sad little collection of mementos and buttons and broken pencils. Smoothing them gently, she had flattened them on the dining room table with one corner of each tucked under the Bilbao tile.

"God, she looks young. I hadn't thought of her as that young ever," David said.

Slightly blurred, as if shaken by giggles, Benita's face was turned toward a young man with a rigid, self-conscious grin.

"That must be Luis. Her boyfriend at the time," Janie explained to the detective. "I'm afraid they won't help you much."

"Every little bit," he murmured. "Her passport picture wasn't exactly taken yesterday either. Still, I'd say it was good luck your finding them. Very good luck." He looked quizzically at Janie before he picked up the photographs and the passport and slipped them between the pages of his notebook.

"There was a baby picture of Aaron, too," Janie told David. "That and the one of her parents were the only other pictures. It seems so little . . . as if her life stopped way back then and nothing else ever happened to her, nothing worth remembering."

"Yeah," Grazzi said. "You don't think she's taken some of her personal things with her?"

"I can't see that she took anything. Anything at all. Not even her hairbrush. David, when we were in there, it didn't look at all as if she'd gone on a trip, you know? There aren't any spaces, or empty hangers. I can't see that she packed anything, and there's a suitcase on the floor of her closet. Her passport was inside."

"Then she can't have gone far," David began.

"Or she was in a terrific hurry."

"Exactly," agreed Grazzi. "Because she was running like hell. The police, Mrs. Ingstrom," he said very clearly, enunciating as if Janie were slow-witted, "do not keep secrets from each other. So let's stop being coy. When you were asked to identify the body, you thought it was your maid's brother, right? You hadn't seen him for a long time, but you were pretty sure."

He took out his notebook again and, careful not to dislodge the photographs, found his place. "A man named Manolo Santos. Benita's brother Manolo. Both of them could've known what was in the tile, right?"

Janie nodded slowly, warily.

"Assuming those jewels were in the tile all the time since

you was a little girl, there weren't too many people around here who necessarily knew about them. Maybe just your maid and her brother . . ."

Intent, staring at Grazzi, Janie continued to nod.

"Your maid and her brother," he repeated distinctly, "and you, Mrs. Ingstrom. You may not want to admit it in the circumstances, but I think you knew all about the tile."

"But I didn't. I told you. If I ever knew, I'd forgotten. When we moved here and I saw it again, I certainly didn't know there were jewels inside. I only knew it came from Bilbao. It says so on it."

Grazzi tucked his notebook back into his pocket, evidently satisfied. "We think it's a new break," he said pleasantly. "Hasn't had time to get dirty, and it's never been glued, anything like that. The jewels couldn't have been safer, if you ask me—until just lately, anyway. And now, well, it looks like we can sort of narrow down our investigation."

"Meaning?" David said, his angry tone covering his uneasiness.

"Meaning it simplifies things when it's more or less all in the family like that."

"Then you're saying that Benny did it. She murdered her brother and ran away."

"It's a possibility. One possibility," Grazzi agreed, but he did not look at David as he answered. His eyes were on Janie, watching her closely. "Those jewels must've been worth fighting about, even worth killing someone for," he said amiably. "It's possible. I don't know your maid. Sisters have been known to clobber their brothers for less. But one thing I do know, Mrs. Ingstrom. You're already on record as hating this guy. You said it yourself. 'I loathed him,' right?"

"God damn it," David burst out, "we weren't anywhere near here. My wife had nothing to do with this."

Grazzi might not have heard him. "Why did you 'loath' him?" he asked Janie.

"Because he was horrible. He was a sneaky little liar. He made me think I'd murdered a man. The man in the picture, in fact. Benita's boyfriend."

"Did you?"

"Of course not. She was a child."

"Mrs. Ingstrom?"

"No." For a moment she seemed incapable of saying anything more. Her hands at her face, she backed away from the detective until she came up against the kitchen door.

"No," she repeated then. "I know what happened now. I found out when we were in Spain. It was Manolo who murdered him and took all the jewels. Almost all," she corrected herself. "Don't you see? Benita had every reason to hate him, even more than I did. They must have got into a fight when he came here, a terrible fight . . ."

Grazzi nodded encouragingly. "Go on, Mrs. Ingstrom, you're doing fine. First you tell me it's the doctor's wife who's behind it, Mrs. Brandt. Now you're trying to pin it on your maid, this Benita. Anyone else?"

"Oh, God," Janie said with horror. "Maybe you're right. Maybe I am going out of my mind. It's all so awful. So unbelievable. And I've been out of my head worrying about Aaron."

It seemed to David that the sound of Aaron's name trig-

146

gered the telephone, and that Janie had the same thought. She was plainly startled, apprehensive, as she backed on through the kitchen door.

"What about him?" were her first words. Then, "Of course I know, Nat. It was my idea. I want to see him. It's all right now. They've cleaned up here."

David was beside her by then and could almost feel the relief, the release of tension that left Janie limp. She put down the receiver and held onto the kitchen counter, her eyes closed.

"Nat. Just making absolutely sure that we really want Aaron back tonight. Meaning," she said bitterly, "absolutely sure that the dear lady is in fit condition to see her son, not screaming her head off. Or," she added as Detective Grazzi filled the doorway, "on her way to jail."

His lips moved judiciously—rather as if he were deciding about a new flavor, David thought—then he shook his head. "Nope. Not tonight anyway," he said blandly. "I still have some work to do, a couple of things to look into."

He seemed unable to pull his eyes away from Janie, however.

"We don't have to talk any more now, do we?" she said. "In front of Aaron?"

"Nope. Not tonight anyway," he repeated.

Chapter 18

They had been away less than a week. A bare seven days, in which the comfortable apartment had been filled with angry currents—flooded and eroded by them, David thought somewhat luridly—and left insidiously changed in every way.

And now here was Aaron, looking subtly different, too, more than a week older and taller. Closely followed by Detective Fitts, he came bursting across the narrow entryway where the body had been. Where Manolo had been; David put a name on it at last, accepting that much.

Janie hesitated perceptibly, long enough to compare this Aaron with her memory of him—and to see that he was wearing his yellow slicker—before she dropped to her knees and hugged him so gratefully that the rubber coat made protesting sounds. Aaron squirmed and wriggled away.

"Hey, hi." David was elaborately casual, rumpling the boy's hair.

"Hi." Aaron looked up solemnly, like a small animal, sensing something.

"My goodness," Janie said quickly, "we hurried back so

fast, we didn't bring you a present. There wasn't time. Baby, I'm sorry."

"Aunt Lynn gave me a present."

"Oh? What?"

"Lots of things," Aaron said.

It was then that the detectives exchanged signals and moved toward the door. "We'll be going along now," Grazzi said.

Passing Aaron, Detective Fitts said, "See you, pal," and punched him lightly.

"You'll be right here. You won't be taking any more trips right away," Grazzi said, and he was not asking, David realized; he was stating a fact.

"You won't mind my going all the way to the deli?"

"You understood me."

When the police were gone, when the apartment was their own again and, superficially at least, back to normal, the full extent of the damage was clear. The familiar rooms felt all wrong. Hostile, gray—David could not define the estranged atmosphere, the antagonism.

"I swear, if I believed in ghosts," Janie said and stopped, conscious of Aaron. Her fingers were clumsy with the buckles on his coat. Fumbling, she backed away from the closet and dropped the coat on a chair. Then, looking determined, drawn and exhausted, she picked up his small suitcase and carried it to his room, switching on lights as she went—all the lights.

"We will need food," David called after her. "Tell me what you want. I'll run down to the deli."

"No, wait. We'll all go." She came rushing back. "And bring up our suitcases. I'd forgotten. If they're still down in the lobby . . ."

Aaron was delighted. This second excursion into the rainy night might have been especially designed as a treat for him. Bedtime had not been mentioned. He pushed his fists through the sleeves of his raincoat without help.

The rain in fact had stopped, and a hustling wind was drying the pavements. Holding hands, Aaron in the middle, they squeezed past other walkers, or strung out, single file, snaked between them, David in the lead pulling and hurrying toward the delicatessen.

Here, briefly, in the briny, smoky warmth of the narrow shop, the nightmare receded. There might never have been a dead man sprawled at their feet. This might have been one of dozens of ordinary nights. Before Benita, they had of necessity taken Aaron almost everywhere with them. He had often jounced along for a mid-evening ice cream or beer, and in the process had developed some exotic tastes. At the moment, somewhat overstimulated, he was showing off, clamoring for herring and macaroni salad.

"No, shrimp instead. I want shrimp," he decided, tired now and shrill. "And a pickle."

The harsh lights showed every weary line in Janie's face, but she was smiling, indulgent, and announced in a surprised voice that she was ravenously hungry. The cheeses and pastrami, sausages, ham and rare roast beef all looked good to her, ambrosial, she said, and took a long time deciding what she most wanted and then, like Aaron, changing her order.

The owner of the delicatessen was a patient man, up to a point. Slicing meats and piling salad into cardboard cartons, he began to mutter about closing time as if he, too, understood that Janie was stalling, spinning out the transaction.

"And lots of pickles!" she said at the end with desperate gaiety. "And hard-boiled eggs. And something for breakfast. Let me think. Orange juice, and we'll need milk. And sweet rolls."

She bought a great deal more than she wanted. David took the bulky sack and heard the door locked with a certain emphasis the moment it closed behind them.

There was no scampering along together now. Slowly as he walked, David found that Janie lagged behind him, gripping Aaron's hand, her face hardened against the wind.

The sidewalks were emptying. Above them the patterns of bright windows suggested snug, safe, normal evenings, people who were glad to be home. Hundreds of them, David thought blackly, all relaxing, putting their feet up and brooding over nice normal problems. Not, as he was, crawling with apprehension. Feeling sick, helpless. And, he might as well admit, scared stiff.

On a surge of anger he turned into their apartment house and with his back against the heavy door, holding it open for Janie and Aaron, he had an instant of pure panic. What he was holding open so politely was an enormous, inescapable trap.

"Won't you step into my parlor?"

"David, don't . . ." Janie's face was pinched tight as she indicated Aaron. In their eagerness to see him, they had forgotten that they would be inhibited by the child's presence, unable to talk about what concerned them most.

So far Aaron seemed untroubled. He went hopping across the tiled lobby on one sneakered foot, enviably oblivious to anything beyond his own immediate concerns. Like the trip to the delicatessen, his visit with the Brandts had been a welcome disruption in his routine, not worth questioning.

Walter, they found, had for once exerted himself to the extent of taking their suitcases upstairs. But not into the apartment; rather pointedly, David felt, he had left them aligned outside their door.

"That's a hell of a place," he said, unlocking the door himself. "Doesn't he have a key?"

Janie nodded. "But he doesn't like to use it. Not unless you specifically ask him to, and then you practically have to put it in writing. He's funny that way, always has been, according to my mother. She wasn't sure if he'd been accused of stealing, or was only afraid he might be."

"Sounds like a guilty conscience to me," said David crossly. "Or he's already got a record and he's running scared."

"Either way I'm afraid he's cautious to a fault. I know what you're thinking, David, but it won't work. I'm sorry. I'm positive that he didn't come in while we were away. He wouldn't have."

"I wish to hell he had."

"I know. This way . . ." Janie paused until sounds from the far end of the hall proved that Aaron was beyond hearing. She took the grocery bag from David then and started through the dining room toward the kitchen. "This way, well, it leaves Benny, doesn't it? There's no one else."

"In an emergency?" David wondered without any real hope. "Wouldn't Walter come in if he thought something was wrong? Say he heard someone inside when no one was supposed to be home, wouldn't he go in then, if he thought someone had broken in?"

Janie doubted it. "That's the thing. He wouldn't want to get involved. He'd call the police. But he wouldn't charge in himself. After all, it's nothing to him. He couldn't have known that the tile was full of goodies."

"No." David thought for a moment and then with a dismal sense of rejecting all the better alternatives repeated, "No." The tile had to be important. The police detectives had carried it off as if it were priceless, a vital—in fact a crucial—piece in their investigation. The motive and the weapon, they had called it, pleased, and David could think of no reason to doubt them. Clearly the man who broke in had known exactly what he was looking for, and that fact alone narrowed the field. Manolo would have known. And Benita. They could easily have been the only ones. Except for Janie; the police assumed that Janie had known about the jewels all along. That Janie . . .

David looked at her anxiously. Her hands were going through fussy, disconnected motions among the packets of meat and the salad cartons. Having opened one flat package to expose rosy strips of pastrami, she very neatly, very absently, folded the white paper back exactly as it had been, closed it again as if the meal were over, or she had had all she wanted. Like a mechanical toy, David thought; she moved like one of Aaron's wind-up toys in the weakening moment before the taut and abused mechanism would let go altogether.

She was working over the macaroni salad now, opening it, closing it. "It has to be Benny. All nice and cozy and in the family like," she mimicked Grazzi. The lid of the container was torn.

"She's the obvious suspect, all right. So she's undoubt-edly innocent. At least in books . . ."

Janie ignored this fatuous statement. "She must have killed Manolo and run away. Poor Benny. Oh, David, in some ways, I hope they never find her."

"Oh, no, you don't, baby. This is one case we want solved. Don't you see? We want to *know* what happened. We've got to. Otherwise . . ." He took Janie's fidgety hands and held them firmly between his own.

Otherwise . . .

There could be worse things than not knowing. He tight-ened his hold protectively.

"David, they can't think it was me. I didn't have anything to do with Manolo's death. This time I know I didn't. The police can't pin it on me."

"Or me?" He had meant to be flippant, but this possibil-ity, now that he had said it aloud, was not funny. "If it boils down to who knew what was in the tile," he said slowly, "and they assume that you always knew . . . why not assume that we all knew? Me, for instance, and your mother and father?"

And Aaron? He had appeared bright-faced in the door-way. There was no way of guessing how much he had heard.

"I want my shrimp now," he said.

Janie spun around and hugged him, her face shiny with tears.

Chapter 19

It was a very bad night, endless, churning, wakeful. Splintered into five and ten minute fragments, David learned whenever he looked at the bedside clock, hoping to prove that he had slept after all and that his muddied, deformed ideas were only dreams. In the incomplete city darkness his mind floundered out of control, to be dragged down by some sinister undertow and tossed among jagged rocks in a boiling white surf.

He had never spent such a night. He would have got up and gone prowling through the apartment, found something to read . . . anything. But a vague revulsion held him down, weighted to the bed. To reach the living room, he would have to pass the hall closet. Manolo had shed a great deal of blood. It would still be in there, dry and caked, but very much there. No one had done anything about it, and now the difficulty of washing away all that blood overwhelmed him.

Queasily he tried to think about something else. Food was no improvement. He blamed the food. He tried to tell himself that ill-advised eating was all that was wrong with him: pastrami and pickles and shrimp. He was not amused. He saw no humor in the pertinent commercials that now haunted him, the animated stomachs and bloated gluttonous faces.

He had eaten mechanically because the food was there, spread out on the kitchen counter among the white wrappings. He remembered Janie biting into an egg, then absently squeezing the slippery remainder until the yoke popped out. Aaron had laughed excessively and mutilated three eggs in an effort to do the same thing. He was clearly overexcited and had stuffed himself, perhaps driven to extreme lengths by his parents' relentless attention.

Janie could not take her eyes off him. What she said, talking rapidly and with hectic gaiety, had very little to do with what she was thinking. David was sure of that as he saw how she watched Aaron, worrying, speculating, trying to guess what he knew.

"Tell me everything that you did while we were away. Everything," she demanded with a terribly forced brightness. "You were going to draw me a fabulous picture, remember!"

"I couldn't make a picture."

"Why not, baby?"

"I didn't have any crayons. Benny forgot my new crayons." He looked around then as if there were something wrong with the kitchen and said, "Where's Benny?"

Janie was cautious. "She had to go away, remember? On a trip."

"Oh. I forgot." His hand hovered undecided between pickles and eggs. "Eeny, meeny, miney, mo . . ."

"Didn't she tell you?" Janie gently persisted. "About her father being sick? Or about her brother? Did you see Benny's brother?"

Aaron shook his head, munching, enwrapped again in his own immediate business.

"Aaron, listen to me." Janie stooped over him, her urgent tone giving the question importance. "There was a tile in the dining room. A Spanish tile, you know the one I mean? It got broken."

Aaron backed away from her. "I didn't do it! I didn't break it!"

"No, I know. I didn't mean you did. I just . . ." Janie had given up and apologized. But Aaron, distrusting her, would not be comforted. When she put out her arms to him, he ran out of the kitchen.

"It's all right. Let him go," David had told her. "It doesn't prove anything. Not necessarily. He just lives in his own little world, that's all. Kids do at that age. They're totally self-centered. It's normal."

Janie was not reassured, or not listening. Like Aaron, she had her own little world.

David could not be sure if Janie ever fell asleep or just lay there in a paralyzed kind of stillness. She had turned away from him. Once, early in the night, he had reached out to her. It was a protective, comforting gesture from which she had recoiled as if the dead man himself had touched her. She had made a tiny, startled sound and then, appalled at herself, said, "Oh, David, darling, how awful! I didn't mean that. It's not you, it's . . . it's everything."

"I know. It's okay." He did not touch her again; she seemed too fragile in this brittle, frozen state.

157

As if she could feel his thoughts on her, she rolled onto her back now, her arms tight against her sides. He could not see if her eyes were open.

"He was here, David," she said as if there had been no hours of silence. "Aaron was here with Benny. They were the only ones." She caught her breath audibly before she said the rest. "What if he does know . . . if he saw what happened?"

"He would have told us."

"Maybe not, if it was too horrible, too shocking to talk about. Or if someone made him promise not to."

For a second David did not understand. And then he did, with the feeling that someone had landed on his stomach with both feet. Janie's whole life had been shadowed by Luis's murder. It couldn't happen again, not to Aaron.

"He seemed okay to me," he argued. "You saw how he ate. He didn't act upset about anything."

"Until I asked him about the tile. He was upset then, enough to run out of the room."

"Because it was broken, and he thought you were accusing him, that's all. That would be bad enough."

"I suppose. Oh, David, I hope you're right." She did not sound convinced, however. Nor comforted.

The early, predawn grind of trucks came as a welcome noise, then the roaring, voracious monsters of the sanitation department. At the first gray preview of morning David eased himself out of bed and pulled on some clothes. Dressed, he thought, he could maneuver better around the grisly closet on his way to the instant coffee.

First thing he would have that mess cleaned up. As soon as he could get police permission, he reminded himself, and wondered about Grazzi's office hours. Did the detective start at nine . . . or stop then, having worked all night? Anyway, the police must have finished whatever business they had in the hall closet. There was no reason why Benita shouldn't get going on it. Benita . . .

He shook himself fully awake. Half his mind had still expected her to slide out of her room as usual, tentatively, in quiet slippers. She would have hesitated to come into the kitchen when he was there, then tactfully she would have taken the kettle out of his hands. He wished to God she would.

Waiting for the water to boil, he snapped on the kitchen radio and rotated the dial in search of voices. News, commercials, all-night talk shows, he didn't care; he only wanted to know that someone else was awake. The day would be windy and cool, partly cloudy—a mediocre Friday, the weatherman called it, but he had high hopes for the weekend, for sunny days and temperatures climbing into the sixties. There had been a derailment, a bomb scare, a UN debate, all kinds of activity in New York and vicinity. The body in the Ingstrom apartment was not mentioned. It was old news—days old now.

With a mug of coffee warm between his hands, David wandered into the living room, waiting for the morning paper to thud down outside the door. He often did this, to be out of Benny's way while she got breakfast—or Janie's in their old apartment. He liked the time alone to sort out his own day.

A mediocre Friday, the man had said. David had always liked Fridays, the wrapping up of the week, the truant mood of the shortened afternoon as the commuters raced to early trains. And left the city to its own, he had often thought, with a proprietary feeling for the abandoned weekend city, the infinite Saturday possibilities and the emptied Sunday streets.

They could rent bicycles in Central Park. Or go skating. Or even take the sightseeing boat around the Island; Aaron would like that. Their week away had sharpened David's appetite for New York. He felt a sudden nostalgia for the things they used to do, a rush of enthusiasm that ended abruptly. Their week away—pushed aside for a moment, the fact snapped back at him all the more brutally—their week away had also landed them in a large can of worms. It was no use pretending that they could get back to normal now.

Until Manolo's death was explained, his murderer caught and the case closed, they would go on as they were: scared, bewildered, suspicious—and suspect. Prize suspects: Grazzi prizing Janie like a cat savoring a mouse, confidently spinning out the game.

Janie of all people. She could no more have killed a man . . . bashed in his head and stuffed him in a closet and left him to die . . . could she? Surely they would be able to establish the time of Manolo's death, to prove once and for all that Janie couldn't have been here, she was in Spain.

David found himself pacing the living room like a wild thing, finding his own company unbearable, and the prospect of the day, the days ahead . . .

The morning was bad enough.

Grazzi could not be reached. David put in a call at half-past seven, and again at close intervals, not trusting messages. The detective was out somewhere, working on a case.

The detective was still out, and so was Detective Fitts.

Aaron came out of his room, barefoot and rumpled, and yawned through a bowl of corn flakes. "Are you going to take me to school?" he said.

"School?" David had forgotten. He managed a spurious sort of jollity. "I think we'll declare a holiday. We'll both stay home. I won't go to the office either. Since we haven't seen each other all week . . ."

As the morning inched along, he began to feel caged, a captive father. Aaron pushed his advantage. Relentlessly he spread out games on the living room floor, squatted down eagerly, and expected David to do the same. Stretched out full length on the rug, propped on one elbow and with one eye on the morning paper, David surmounted the frustrations of Chutes and Ladders. He was skunked at Concentration, however. His mind skittered away from the cards—to the closet, to Grazzi. And to something else that nagged and carped at the very edge of his consciousness. Something missing, something he had forgotten to do?

At any other time Janie would have been amused by Aaron's victories. She drifted around them, back and forth through the apartment, wanly busying herself.

"I loathe unpacking," she said once. "Everything looks so abused . . . so disenchanted somehow."

"You want to trade places?" David rearranged his cramped legs, wondering if they would support him.

"No, no. That's done. I've got some calls to make." She went back to the bedroom.

There was an invalid atmosphere. David remembered measles, and the long shut-in weekend they had all spent with Aaron's chicken pox.

"I beat you, I beat you!" Aaron scooped up the last matched pairs, full of himself. "Let's play that again."

"Your son," he told Janie on her next transit, "has a phenomenal memory."

"Oh?"

"For cards."

"Oh, I see." She looked bleak again. "I've been talking to Dody."

"And?" He straightened his glasses.

"She's terribly upset. Naturally. She didn't know if she should call us or not. Or what." Janie glanced toward Aaron—he was shuffling the cards in his own way, smearing them around on the rug—and she went on guardedly. "They've been there, checking our story. They've gone over and over it with her."

"I hope they're satisfied."

Janie nodded miserably. "She couldn't add much either. She repeated just what she'd told us before, except for one thing. She did notice an odd smell when she was here. She didn't want to say anything at the time. But it means that he . . ." Janie's eyes moved to Aaron, "*it* must have been in the closet then."

"What does Grazzi say to that?"

"Oh, he agrees. He thinks it had been there a couple of days by then, at least. He hasn't had a final report on the autopsy, but they're estimating the time of death as sometime Monday."

"Then, no problem!" David sat up with a surge of relief. "We were in Madrid. That's easy enough to verify."

"I think he already has. The thing is," eyeing Aaron, she had trouble with the words, "in this case, the time of death doesn't necessarily prove much. He was alive when he was put in there. It seems that's what counts, when he was locked in."

"Oh, Lord."

"And," Janie said tightly, "it also seems that Detective Grazzi is fascinated by me. He thinks I'm holding out on him. And he asked Dody a lot of questions, about my emotional stability . . . and things."

"Janie . . ." David's hands rose then fell back with a sense of enormous weight.

That was what he remembered best about the morning—the gray, leaden, sinking feeling . . . being dragged down, deeper and deeper, helplessly. And the persistent feeling that he was overlooking something—something important.

Chapter 20

Grazzi got back to them in the afternoon, late, giving them maximum time to wonder and speculate—and suffer, David concluded, as if this were some form of psychological warfare and the detective had deliberately left them alone to torture themselves. Confined in solitary long enough, he wondered, would the prisoner welcome his captor? Would any change look better to him than this limbo, this ignorance? *Almost* anything.

Daytime television—the sufferings of soap opera and giveaway shows—did not hold his attention, and he wondered what Aaron saw in them. Or was he, too, merely staring blindly while his mind raced elsewhere?

David had slipped off to find Janie. She was perched on a high stool at the kitchen counter, her legs wrapped among the rungs, pencil in hand, but she had written nothing on the narrow pad in front of her.

"Anything we need, I'll be glad to go get it," he said.

She was not with him. "There must be a way. There's got to be," she said.

He waited. The canned voices droned on in the living room. "I'm sure Aaron can't hear us. A way to what?"

She looked startled. "To prove we didn't do it, any of us!" she said passionately. "And I thought of something. David . . ." She lowered her voice. "If they can't be sure when Manolo was locked in the closet. If it's give or take a day or two . . ."

"You wouldn't be eyeing the night of our party? It won't work, baby. I'm sorry, but we were all here together, you know, the Brandts and the Emmets and us. Anyway, Manolo wasn't in the closet when you and I left. We would have noticed when we took out our coats." He smiled thinly, but Janie missed the grim humor in this.

She seemed to crumple, not just her face but her whole body and her resolve. "It always comes back to me. Benny and me. What if they can't find Benny?"

"I think maybe I'd better find us a lawyer." Even then he could not attach the word "criminal"; it would have sounded too melodramatic . . . silly.

When at last, late in the afternoon, the door buzzer was pushed, twice, lightly, Janie spun around on the stool. "Benny?"

For those few seconds she could hope so, until they arrived in the hallway and David opened the door.

The large detective had the look of a man who had put in a long and unrewarding day: exhausted, wrinkled, resentful. Detective Fitts stood slightly behind him, a small version of the same.

In the awkward pause David went on the offensive. "I've been trying to reach you."

"Oh? I've been around. A lot of places," Grazzi volunteered unpleasantly. "Something you wanted to tell me?"

"No, ask. Nothing important." Grazzi's manner stopped him; the gruesome closet was diminished after all to a minor housekeeping problem. Grazzi's eyes, squinting and red-veined with fatigue, moved back and forth with more than a hint of contempt.

"I don't suppose you've heard from your maid," he said.

"No. Just for a minute, just now, I thought you might be Benny. But"—Janie faltered under the detective's stare—"I suppose she'd use her own key."

Grazzi nodded, not in agreement, but sarcastically, as if Janie's answer was only to be expected. He pushed on into the living room then, snapped off the television set and lowered himself onto the arm of an upholstered chair. "You might as well sit down," he told them, and waited until they had.

Aaron's mouth fell open, but he did not protest, and recognizing Detective Fitts, he managed a tentative smile.

Fitts, David noticed, stayed near the door, on the edge of one of those spindly chairs that men usually avoid. He did not return Aaron's smile.

Grazzi clearly was going to take his time. When everyone was seated, he rubbed his eyes and let the silence stretch nervously, like a rubber band, almost to breaking point. "Maybe you want the little boy out of here," he said then.

"Yes. Of course. Come on, darling. Time to go play in your own room." Janie started to get up.

"Just the kid," Grazzi said.

"Okay, Mrs. Ingstrom," he went on when Aaron was gone. "Do you want to change your story now? Or later?"

"I don't understand."

"I think you do."

Again Grazzi was noticeably silent, unhurried. Again David thought of psychological warfare as perfected by a large, sadistic cat. Janie seemed to have no defenses.

"Or maybe I didn't hear you right." Grazzi snorted gently, and the arm of his chair responded as he shifted his weight, settling into his subject. "I got the impression that you had this Spanish woman working for you, woman by the name of Benita Santos, right?"

Janie nodded, lost.

"And this maid of yours had a brother name of Manolo. Who turned up dead. Out there." His chin jutted toward the hall. "At least that was my impression from what you said. Do correct me if I'm wrong."

He was suddenly snide, affected, crudely impersonating a woman while he glared at Janie. "You did identify the victim as Manolo Santos? You built up a pretty good case against the sister, too, while you were at it . . . handed me a ready-made motive. Bad blood from way back . . . the two of them fighting over the jewels. And the lady clearing out, running away, looking guilty as hell. Sure. Cock-and-bull story about her hotfooting it back to Spain. I gotta hand it to you, it was a good try. But . . .

"To start with, obviously—you'll agree on this—she didn't go nowhere near Spain without her passport."

"I didn't say she did. I didn't say she went to Spain. That was what I was told. It's what Mrs. Brandt said Benny said, that she had to go to Spain because we'd called her about her father being sick . . ."

Grazzi let her struggle for a minute, then he smiled. "Uh-huh. At least that was your story. Very clever. Organizing her disappearance to make her the number-one suspect."

"But I didn't call her!" Janie frantically battled his disbelief. "We were in Spain by then. We didn't know about any of this . . ."

"They tell me they have phones in Spain, too, these days . . . and you sure gave 'em a workout. We've looked into that by making a few calls ourselves." Grazzi was pleased with himself. "We looked into a lot of things, in fact, Mrs. Ingstrom, and we discovered some other things about your story. One thing you had right: Spanish national Manolo Santos did come into this country, arriving New York October second. There's just one slight hitch."

Tight-faced, her mouth clamped shut, Janie seemed to be holding her breath.

"The catch is"—Grazzi paused cruelly—"he also departed New York. Last week, in good health as far as anybody knows, on a plane to Lisbon. After that, we've lost him for now, but never mind. The main thing is he's not the stiff in your closet. So why'd you hand me that guff?"

Janie seemed to be holding herself together by digging her fingernails into her clenched arms. She did not answer.

"You want I should guess? I'd say it was a mighty fancy way to save your own skin. You kill a guy—or your husband does, reasons of your own—let your maid take the rap. Beautiful. She's not too bright maybe, doesn't speak much English. Makes it easier, especially when she's not around to defend herself. There's just one little part I haven't figured out yet. How'd you get her to disappear really? You got her stashed away somewhere, too? Like permanently shut up?"

"That's enough!" It came out as a bark, hoarse with fury,

168

and David was out of his chair, standing in front of Janie as if to shield her from this barrage of words.

"Don't listen to him," he told her. "And don't say anything more. Not until we've got help. We're getting a lawyer."

"I'd do that if I were you," Grazzi said amiably. "For the both of you. I can wait."

"David . . ." Janie clung to him. She went with him to the telephone in the kitchen and huddled against him while he looked up a number and, freeing his arm with some difficulty, dialed it.

"David, what are we going to do?"

He put his finger against her lips and pressed the receiver closer to his ear to hear. Awkwardly, with Janie crowding his arm, he wrote down the name and number he had been given and dialed again.

"What if they arrest us?" Janie said the instant he hung up. "Don't let them."

He put his arms around her. "We'll raise bail . . . or something. This man Porter will know what to do. Alan Porter. He deals in this sort of thing all the time. He'll know."

Stroking Janie, reassuring her, he repeated the words in a voice that was not his own.

She drew back to see his face.

He looked away.

No matter what he said, the uncertainty remained. He looked down at Janie then and saw his own fear reflected. As if she was thinking what he was thinking. "There's got to be a way out," he said.

"All I can think of is running, getting out of here. That's

what I feel like, running away."

"Except that there's Aaron."

"I know. But what if we are arrested, David? What will happen to him then?"

"Come on," he said, and with one arm still around her he led her out of the kitchen and through the dining room. In the hall, in full view of the living room, they abruptly stopped.

The room was empty, the detectives gone.

"What the devil . . . !"

Janie signaled to him to be quiet and, listening, they heard a mumble of low voices . . . from Aaron's room.

Janie did not hesitate. She went down the hall well ahead of him and seemed to flash around the corner, bristling and dangerous, instinctively protective.

"Don't you dare. Don't you touch him," she warned.

The bedroom door was open. Detective Fitts stood leaning against it. The other one, Grazzi, sat heavily on the edge of the little boy's bed, so weighing down the mattress that Aaron had slid down cozily beside him.

"Leave my son out of this," Janie said. "You have no right!"

Neither of the men moved. Nor did Aaron. Whatever David had expected to find, it was not this, this congenial group. They might have been interrupted at some game, and Aaron—winning again?—was clearly charmed by his new playmates.

"No right to question him behind my back!" Janie faltered.

Stolid, impervious, Grazzi said, "Your son has been a big help." He glowered at Janie through another of his calculated silences, returning her mistrust.

"Maybe a very big help," he added at last. "I was asking him about your maid. About the last time he saw her. I thought it might give us something to go on."

"Children have no sense of time. He wouldn't know."

"That's not quite what I asked him, Mrs. Ingstrom. I was more interested in the circumstances, like did she tell him good-bye. Seems she didn't."

Grazzi paused ominously, but this time Janie said nothing. "Seems there was something about a letter though. Would you know about that?"

"Aunt Lynn told me." Aaron bounced on the bed. "I'm going to get a letter!"

"Or someone is. Or did," Grazzi said, questioning Janie, his eyes never leaving her. "I thought maybe there was a slight misunderstanding in there. Or you were holding out on me again?"

"Good Lord!" David exploded, pounding himself with a suddenness that brought him the full, startled attention of both the detectives. "That's what's been bugging me all day, what's been missing," he said. "The mail. We never picked up our mail. With everything else going on . . ."

"It's no wonder," Fitts said mildly, accompanying him to the elevator.

Chapter 21

The week's accumulation of mail jammed the box, so tightly that several edges were torn as David pulled them out. There was a preponderance of junk mail, some bills. Riffling through, he at last came to one, a plain cheap white envelope, addressed to Janie in an unsteady handwriting that might be Benita's.

Before it was removed from his hands, he saw that it was slightly smudged and had been postmarked in New York.

"I'll take that," Detective Fitts said. He carried it upstairs with a gingerly sort of tenderness.

With the same care and closely witnessed by his fellow officer, he slit it open. They had moved back to the living room, Grazzi and Janie, and Aaron was not sent out of the room this time. Janie held him close to her, letting him squirm, not releasing him.

For a long moment Grazzi and Fitts puzzled over the letter together, and Grazzi was skeptical still when he looked up. "If this is for real," he said.

"If . . . " he repeated, "then it looks like a full confession. The Spanish woman. Says she found this man in your apartment . . . and she killed him. Then she couldn't stand what she'd done, so she was going to kill herself."

Janie caught her breath audibly and held Aaron even more tightly. "Oh, how awful . . . poor Benny." There were tears welling in her eyes.

Grazzi watched her closely, gauging her reaction. "You think she'd do a thing like that?"

Janie nodded, her eyes closed, seeping tears.

"On the other hand"—Grazzi looked tough again—"it's such a lucky break for you, it strikes me, it couldn't be better if you'd written the letter yourself. You didn't by any chance, did you, Mrs. Ingstrom?"

Janie shook her head wordlessly.

"Well, easy enough to check out the handwriting. We've got experts . . ."

The door buzzer cut harshly through what he was saying. Detective Fitts responded instantly.

A deep, serious, unfamiliar voice said, "Mr. Ingstrom? My name is Porter. Alan Porter."

David grinned uncontrollably into the long, stern face of the lawyer. "With any luck," he said, "I've misled you. Got you here under false pretenses. Or false alarms. Up the garden path on a wild goose chase and all that. So sue me! What I mean is, I don't think we'll be needing you."

He was light-headed, garrulous, silly. Drunk with relief.

Chapter 22

It was not a party exactly. Three days later Janie was still noticeably subdued, pale, saddened by the thought of Benita's death, but she wanted to see her old friends. So the Emmets had come, Dody laden with lasagna, and the Brandts had brought a gallon of Chianti. Aaron rolled black olives on the rug as before, as if it were a party.

Lynn Brandt ruffled his hair. "Hey, chum. We've missed you. You can come visit anytime."

"Oh, Lynn, I'm so sorry," Janie began unsteadily, not for the first time. "All those awful things I thought . . . I was out of my mind. I can't tell you . . ."

Lynn laughed kindly. "Then will you please stop trying! It's over, forgotten, I'm not the least bit offended. And I don't blame you! Dear Janie, with all the hideous things that were happening, it's no wonder."

Still smiling, she let her hand rest lightly on Aaron's shoulder. "I just hope mine's as nice."

"Your what?" asked David from behind a trayful of drinks.

Nat Brandt inflated his chest. "Son and heir, that's what. What else?"

"Lynn!" Janie hugged her. "Honestly?"

"I've been holding my breath. It seemed like tempting fate if I told anybody, but . . . yes! So if I've been a little secretive . . . well, now you know."

David raised his glass ceremonially. "And while we're up, I'd like to publicly rescind a few sinister opinions of my own. My apologies, Nat. I'm afraid I thought insanity was contagious, sort of an occupational hazard in your profession."

Nat roared with laughter and said, "Cheers!"

"To friendship," Don Emmet proposed, and they drank together.

"And all that time," Dody said, her eyes wide over the rim of her glass, "it was Benny, all by herself, poor thing. Can you imagine how lonely she must have been, doing all that, then going off to die," Dody shuddered, "in the river?"

"That's the police theory anyway," David put in, "since there's no trace of her. When someone vanishes that completely, well . . ." He sipped his drink gratefully. "Anyway, there's no doubt about her confession, thank God for that. The writing was definitely Benny's. It checked out with the signature in her passport and a couple of lists in her room."

"I always said you were lucky, didn't I?"

"There've been times when I might have argued with you," he said dryly.

"Well, yes," Dody conceded. "Your trip can't have been much fun. But"—she brightened immediately—"you can always go back!"

"Oh, no." It was Janie, sliding close to him, her arm

around his waist. "I don't think so. I've had my childhood, thank you." She looked up at David sunnily. "Unless you're still hankering for those dancing girls. Shall we tell her the rest?"

David shrugged.

"Okay. My parents want their apartment back, isn't it marvelous! They want to come back east. We're being evicted. Any vacancies in your neighborhood?"

"You're kidding. You must be out of your mind!"

Janie beamed. "No more."

Dody eyed her with grave suspicion. "I think I'll go see if the lasagna is hot yet."

. . . Later

The tide was out so that the beach was at its widest, and there was a broad compacted hem where three children were running, ducking, doubling back like sea gulls at some intricate game. The woman watched them with a vague, tolerant pleasure. She walked slowly along the paved path at the upper edge of the sand.

The man behind her had been following her for some time, at a distance, still not sure and above all not wanting to frighten her away. When at last he decided that the time had come, that he must speak to her, he closed the distance very gradually and spoke her name softly.

"Benita?"

She turned, alarmed.

"Then it is you," he said. "It's all right," he added quickly, because she was frightened after all. Terrified. He had not expected such a degree of shock.

"It's all right," he said again. "Please don't run. I won't hurt you. I only want to talk to you."

She was confused now, shaken still but curious. It was

evident that she had expected to see someone else—someone she was afraid of.

"I'm the one who calls himself Luis. Luis Varga," he said. She nodded slowly, recognizing him.

"I'm sorry. Please forgive me."

"It doesn't matter." She shrugged, then unexpectedly smiled, not a resigned, sad smile but one with a hint of merriment. "Who knows what Luis would have thought?"

"At the time, I didn't think about that. It was necessary to use his identity, that's all. I didn't kill him, you know. Your brother did."

"I know. I always knew that. And I don't blame you for doing what you did. In your place, I would have done the same." She paused, looking closely at his face, and seemed to come to a favorable decision.

"Yes, exactly the same," she said then. She looked away, her eyes following the line of the breakwater out to the open mouth of the bay, then turned back to him suddenly in her eagerness to explain. "What I did *was* the same. You see, when Manolo was dead, to get away I had to take his identity. His passport, his pocketbook, even his coat and hat, I took. Everything. You understand, there was no Benita any more."

"In the same way that there was no Brock. Exactly. I understand."

"I killed him," she went on, speaking earnestly, as if it were important that he understand everything. "I don't know if I meant to kill him. But I think that he had to die. Before he did more bad things, I had to stop him.

"You see, Manolo knew that you had given to Janie some jewels long ago. He was greedy. When all the rest were gone, he wanted hers, too. He came to New York."

Benita closed her eyes, reliving the time when Manolo had reappeared, like an evil shadow over her life, spying on her, always calling her on the telephone, always threatening, waiting to do harm.

"What he didn't know," she said after a minute, "was that Janie had lost the jewels. They meant nothing to a child. She had tossed them aside. I found them by the path. That path." She looked back over her shoulder with an air of surprised recognition.

"I hid them. In a tile I had. I gouged out little secret pockets and stuck them inside and covered them again with the felt. All those years, they were safe there. Nobody suspected. They were all I had."

"But in the end Manolo got those, too?"

Grimly Benita nodded. "But he did not have them for long," she said with some satisfaction.

"He waited for me that morning in the hall outside the apartment, just by the door, so that when I came out to take the little boy to school, he caught at the door. He did not let it close, and he pretended that he had come to wash the windows, so that the boy thought nothing.

"I had to go on to the school. Still, I thought the jewels were safe. He searched everywhere while I was gone. Perhaps he recognized the tile and broke it in his anger. Anyway, he found what he wanted.

"And he was furious because there was not more! He waited for me. He demanded the rest. He had expected to find a great fortune. He *needed* it, he said."

Agitated, gesticulating, her whole body involved in this account, Benita moved passionately along the walk.

Brock quietly kept up with her. "But he could not expect you to . . . to finance him. Surely not."

"No. Not I. But Janie and her husband, and her parents; they must all be rich, he thought. He would have their money, he said."

"I don't quite see how."

"There was the little boy. Aaron. If he took Aaron, Manolo said, they would give him all their money fast enough . . ."

Tears filled Benita's eyes as she said this, and she brushed them away furiously. "That's when I struck him. The tile was the nearest thing. It was sharp where he had broken it. His neck and his head, he was bleeding a great deal, and I left him in the closet to die."

"That was a brave thing."

"No, a terrible thing. I murdered him."

"Perhaps not so bad. In defense . . ." Then in a spontaneous gesture—of support, of approval; he could not have explained—Brock offered his arm to Benita, and she, as unconsciously, slipped her arm through his. "And then?" he asked.

"I cleaned the apartment, everything. Still I could not bring the little boy back there, of course, with the body. I took him to Janie's friends. And then, when I could think, I knew that I was in terrible trouble. When they found Manolo, everyone would know what I had done. And I knew what I must do . . .

"First, quickly, I took everything from his pockets. Everything, as I told you, so that nobody would know who he was. Later I found that somehow I had missed the emerald. But all his money and identifications I had."

"But what about Janie, when she came back? Wouldn't she recognize Manolo?"

"I thought she might guess. We resembled each other very much, Manolo and I. But she could never be sure. She was a child when she saw him."

"Even then . . ." Brock scowled, worrying. "Could she be blamed? When the body was found in her apartment . . . ?"

"I thought about that. I didn't want her to suffer. So I wrote a letter. A confession. I said that I was responsible for the man's death, and therefore there would be no more Benita."

Her smile flickered. "They would think I had killed myself, no? I did not tell an exact lie. But they would not look for me any more. And then I came back here, as Manolo. I used his passport, his beret even!

"And I am here," she concluded, her hands spread wide, emptied.

"Yes." Brock nodded, approving. "You did the right thing."

They had moved perhaps half the way along the edge of the beach toward the breakwater.

"Just about here," Brock said, "is where I landed. I'll never forget it."

"Nor will I."

"And I often think of Janie, the way she was then."

"Yes. So do I. Chainee, I called her." Benita smiled, remembering Janie's fury, her little heels digging into the sand and her face blazing. *Can't you even say my name right!*

Also published by MILTON HOUSE BOOKS

Masquerade in Venice
by Velda Johnston

Venice in the 1880's. To the great Belzoni family house on the Grand Canal flees penniless governess Sara Randall who leaves her New England home under a cloud. There she hopes to find a livelihood as paid companion to the great aunt she has never met, the aged Contessa Belzoni. She also hopes to escape the memory, not only of an accusing-eyed coroner's jury back in Connecticut, but of a love that had ended in bitter words and a broken engagement.

However, soon after her arrival a near fatal 'accident' gave rise to her bewildered suspicion that someone in the household regarded her with murderous hostility.

Sara becomes unmistakably aware of the lethal web someone has woven around her. Forbidden by the police to leave Venice, she knows that her only hope of freedom, and perhaps of life itself, lies in finding the weaver of the web.

Here, set in the baroque splendour of Venice, is a novel that blends Gothic terror with an absorbing love story.

192 pages.   **£2.30 net**

The late Mrs Fonsell
by Velda Johnston

The great tragedy-haunted Fonsell house looms over the New England port of Sag Harbour which is growing in prosperity in the 1870's. Had Irene Haverly ever known that some day she would be the mistress of the house she would have been appalled. However, circumstances force her to enter into a marriage of convenience with ambitious Jason Fonsell whose own life is clouded by the violent and unexplained death years before of Julia Fonsell, his beautiful young stepmother.

Soon after Irene enters its ugly portals as Jason's unloved and unloving bride, the Fonsell house is again visited by sudden death. Who is the killer and what link can there be between this new tragedy and the mysterious murder of the past? Only as long as she does not know the answers is Irene's own life safe.

Here, set in a historic whaling village and on a colourful Caribbean island, is a spellbinding tale of Gothic horror and romance.

224 pages.   **£2.30 net**

Miranda
by Celia Larner

'Could you possibly look after the baby for a couple of weeks? . . . . Don't worry, you couldn't possibly know less about babies than I do. Love, Janie. P. S. Her name is Miranda'.

Oliver ignoring his friends' advice that he should hand the child straight over to the police takes her in, it was only for a fortnight after all. The weeks become months and the months become years and gradually Miranda becomes Oliver's life.

Author Celia Larner has written a compassionate and moving story about the formative years of a child and the problems confronting the young artist who decided to bring her up.

248 pages

£2.00 net

Also published by MILTON HOUSE BOOKS

The Italian Maze
by Esme Lascelles

Through a chance encounter with an Indian prince who has come to live next door to her family's home in Essex, Creenagh Elliott gets involved in a fight for her life.

She is invited to Italy to stay with a Marchese who wants her to mend her valuable porcelain collection. Soon, however, Creenagh realises that someone is out to kill her. But who, and above all, why?

Creenagh's relief when her boy friend, Nicky Stacey, appears quickly turns to alarm when she begins to suspect his motives. She finds herself caught in a web of suspicion and intrigue.

This is an exciting, light-hearted thriller with plenty of pace and local colour and a gripping series of climaxes.

160 pages.   **£1.80 net**

Also published by **MILTON HOUSE BOOKS**

The Broken Key

by Mary Linn Roby

Penarth is a great estate towering over the rugged
Cornish coastline. It is owned by the eccentric Randolph
family and when artist Sara Grey, who had been a
companion to the tyrannical owner's sister, arrived to
claim a cottage willed to her in death by the woman, she
is trapped in a bitter family feud. For her benefactress
had been estranged from the Randolphs, and by leaving
Sara the property old wounds are reopened.

The Randolphs are fanatically determined to
repossess the cottage and Sara, after finding that a
young Randolph daughter fell to her death from the cliffs,
begins to fear for her safety.

She finds herself involved in a cycle of terror and
tension, madness and unrequited love, that threatens her
peace of mind and her life.

224 pages.

£2.30 net

Also published by **MILTON HOUSE BOOKS**

Laura Possessed
by Anthea Fraser

'Ahead of them lay a large, pleasant hall, bright and welcoming but, without warning a sudden, choking feeling of terror flooded over her ... in that instant she was overpoweringly aware of an almost tangible wave of despair emanating from the house, making her gasp as its cold desolation seeped through her.'

Laura possessed ... slowly, tormented by the soul of a dead woman, Noel, whose object is to rediscover the lover who was the cause of her death. But for what reason, for love or for revenge?

Laura Hardy, lately recovered from an accident and staying with her brother Edward in the country is, by any standards, an ordinary enough young girl if somewhat literary. Now she finds herself in the grip of an experience, unearthly certainly, perhaps demoniacal, that she cannot control and which affects in various startling ways the lives of those around her, not least her own family.

Laura possessed is a chilling study of a psychic phenomenon brilliantly interpreted by the remarkable talent of Anthea Fraser.

240 pages.   £2.30 net